PENGUIN METRO READS

# HOLD MY HAND

DURJOY DATTA was born in New Delhi, and completed a degree in engineering and business management before embarking on a writing career. His first book—*Of Course I Love You . . .*—was published when he was twenty-one years old and was an instant bestseller. His successive novels—*Now That You're Rich . . .*; *She Broke Up, I Didn't!*; *Oh Yes, I'm Single!*; *You Were My Crush . . .*; *If It's Not Forever . . .*; *Till the Last Breath . . .*; *Someone Like You*; *Hold My Hand*; *When Only Love Remains*; *World's Best Boyfriend*; *Our Impossible Love*; and *The Girl of My Dreams*—have also found prominence on various bestseller lists, making him one of the highest-selling authors in India.

Durjoy also has to his credit nine television shows and has written over a thousand episodes for television.

Durjoy lives in Mumbai. For more updates, you can follow him on Facebook (www.facebook.com/durjoydatta1) or Twitter (@durjoydatta) or mail him at durjoydatta@gmail.com.

# Hold My Hand

# DURJOY DATTA

Penguin
metro reads

PENGUIN METRO READS

USA | Canada | UK | Ireland | Australia
New Zealand | India | South Africa | China

Penguin Metro Reads is part of the Penguin Random House group of companies
whose addresses can be found at global.penguinrandomhouse.com

Published by Penguin Random House India Pvt. Ltd
7th Floor, Infinity Tower C, DLF Cyber City,
Gurgaon 122 002, Haryana, India

Penguin
Random House
India

First published in Penguin Metro Reads by Penguin Books India 2013

Copyright © Durjoy Datta 2013

All rights reserved

20  19  18  17  16  15  14

This is a work of fiction. Names, characters, places and incidents are either the
product of the author's imagination or are used fictitiously and any resemblance
to any actual person, living or dead, events or locales is entirely coincidental.

ISBN 9780143420903

Typeset in Bembo Roman by SÜRYA, New Delhi
Printed at Replika Press Pvt. Ltd, India

www.penguin.co.in

*To the great cities of Delhi and Hong Kong*

# Part One

# The Nerd Boy

1

When I was a little child, I could squeeze between the tiny bookracks where no books would dare find a space, with my favourite Roald Dahl book, and stay there till the end of Dad's shift, away from the bullies, protected from people who didn't appreciate books—I have grown up sitting in such secret places. In the last decade, I have gained inordinate height, though my weight has remained constant, making me resemble a praying mantis—tall, gangly, awkward and strange with spectacled eyes. Mom thinks I am beautiful.

Today, I sit in the corner, almost embarrassed, my extraordinarily long legs folded awkwardly under the chair as I read my favourite Henner Jog book for the thirteenth time this year.

The table I sit on is engraved with the names of my favourite authors and poets and lines from books I have read. When younger, I would scratch out the name of every book I would read with a compass. I stopped when I realized that all books, like all writers, aren't equally good, and Dad slapped me and told me that I wasn't supposed to destroy library property. The word 'destroy' stuck in my head—and I wondered if by engraving names of books and writers that I didn't actually like any more or would recommend anyone to read, would destroy anything.

Now, I use permanent markers, which are anything but permanent, and I continually remove the names and the writers I wouldn't want anyone else to read.

Indraprastha Book Library was set up in 1926; its best days behind it, now its patrons are mostly old people who still look for books that are long forgotten and out of print. In all probability, one can find the book here, given they have the requisite patience to find it amongst the 300,000,000 books and journals and magazines stacked and piled and racked in the six hundred shelves spread over four floors. The library still uses an archaic cataloguing software that hardly works.

Dad is still at his desk, and I figure I have four more hours to finish the book (I know I will finish it in two).

'Namaste, Deep, reading the same book again?' Asha, a woman of fifty-two years, who has been working here almost as long as Dad, smiles her toothy smile and asks. She wipes the floor with a wet rag, but the floor doesn't dry up easily because the ceiling is too high and the fan above rotates with painful slowness.

I nod and say, 'There are not many books around here,' and she smiles at the irony, and she gets back to her mopping, and I get back to my book. It's about a father and a little girl and the road trip they go on after her mother dies in an accident. It's tragic, but it's also funny and beautiful, like all good books are. I always cry reading the book, not when the mother dies but when they order for three people at a pit-stop and the girl takes the third plate and eats from it and says, 'I am growing up. I need food!'

'It's time,' Dad says peering over my shoulder; I am darkening the name HENNER JOG on the table.

'I intend to rub it off some day,' I answer, guilty even though it's been ten years since the Compass Engraving incident.

'It's okay, no one comes to this part of the library any more. All kids want to do is go behind the racks and—' Dad stops mid-sentence seeing me blush.

'Did you read anything good today?' he asks and I point to the book and Dad smiles, out of occasion, like the father in the book smiles at the daughter.

We leave the floor and walk to the elevator—the kind that looks like a wrought-iron cage, the kind of elevator people get stuck in and die—and exit the building. I wave to an autorickshaw, Dad haggles and the auto driver curses the fuel prices.

'Did Maa call you?' I ask.

'Yes, she did. Is she still angry with you? She told me she has made *aaloo poshto* and *doi maachh*. I think you should meet her halfway,' Dad says, trying to be the calm pacifist.

'She can't bribe me with food! Although I have to accept that she has made the right move towards reconciling with me, but like every expert negotiator, I will bide my time and sit this one out,' I say and think about dinner. My mouth waters with anticipation. It's strange how much I love food and yet how excruciatingly thin I am.

'If only you could be an expert negotiator and save us some money on these auto rides back home,' Dad mocks.

'Whatever. I am just angry that you are on her side,' I retort.

'She's gorgeous and she cooks great food, when you're just a tall, lanky boy who's only useful to change fused light bulbs,' he laughs and flips to the page he had bookmarked before and starts reading even as the shaky auto threatens to knock the book out of his hands. It's a poetry book by Rabindranath Tagore, and like every Bengali, he is devoted to the irritatingly multi-talented man.

It's awfully quiet at dinner, till the voices of the distraught housewives in the Bengali serial fill up the bedroom. Mom is at one side of the bed, hardly eating. I am on the other, my plate resting on the day's newspaper, which is spread across the bed.

'Have you decided?' she asks, her eyes fixed on the television.

'Yes, Maa . . .' I declare. 'I have to go. It's a once in a lifetime opportunity. I can't just let it go because you think I will die hungry or get kidnapped!' I protest.

'Do whatever you want to do, why do you ask me anything then?' she grumbles and eats, her nostrils flared, cheeks flushed.

'It's not a big deal, Mamoni. He will go there for a few days and come back. It's a very short project, isn't it? They are asking him to code a software for cataloguing for libraries. It's exciting for him!' Dad says and pats Mom's back.

'I don't know,' she answers, blinking her tears away, shaking her head.

'There is nothing to worry about, baba,' Dad assures Mom. 'They will take good care of him, I am sure. Plus, he is all grown up. For God's sake, he's taller than both of us put together!'

Mom starts crying, and in the next instant, in the blink of an eye, like an invisible ninja, is next to me, hugging me, drowning me in her tears, kissing me, wailing all the while. I am an only child, protected and loved beyond what is healthy for any kid to be, because parents die and then one has to go on road trips—just like it happened in the book I read this morning.

'You will go so, so far away, babu. Why do you have to go? Can't you just stay here and do something? What will I do without you? And what if something happens to you?' Mom sobs, her tears wetting her face and mine.

'I will be okay there, Maa. We will always be in touch over the phone! It's not like the olden days. Remember technology? It'll keep us connected constantly,' I assure her. 'And if the project ends early, I will come back.'

'Who will feed you there?' she asks and smothers me in a hug again, and then makes a small ball of rice and fish and puts it in my mouth. 'You will grow so weak!'

'Weaker than this?' I respond and my father laughs; I weigh fifty-eight kilograms and I am six feet three inches, my waist worth the envy of runway models.

She cries some more at this, the serial ends, and we eat; Mom keeps blinking away her tears, and I daydream about cataloguing algorithms for libraries that would allow the books I like to be easily discovered, allowing me to slip in my own recommendations, quite like the desk in the library with book names engraved on it, only in binary and inside the computer.

But I hope not to destroy.

# 2

I am a really bad sketch artist. All the people in my sketches look nearly alike. They all have crooked noses and slender bodies, the buildings always lean to the right, the birds and the bees are always dots and scratches, and yet I sketch, when I am extraordinarily bored. Not because I don't like the Advanced JAVA class in all its binary glory, but because I know it too well.

'What are you sketching?' Manasi asks. She is texting furiously on her iPhone. It's new and has a glittery case with a picture of the five boys, who look alike and call themselves One Direction, on it, and the screen is crowded with applications.

'I'm not sketching, I'm doodling,' I lie.

'Dude, you're licking your lips and your concentration is like a sniper's. You're definitely sketching!' she says, looking up momentarily, and then gets back to texting. 'I really love the touch response of this phone. And your sketching is really bad, like *really bad*!'

'Thank you for the confidence in my work. You're a true friend,' I say and put the pencil down. At least she's honest.

'And who are you texting anyway?' I ask. 'It's not like you have any friend other than me.'

'Oh shut up! I have Aman,' she protests.

'Aman doesn't text you,' I say, looking around. 'Where is he, by the way?'

'I don't know. He must be with his bimbo girlfriend, who cares?' she says. 'You know what? Yesterday I saw this really cute boy running on the adjacent treadmill and he kept looking at me, and then I kept looking at him, and then he ran faster and faster and looked at me and I wondered whether he was trying to run away from me!' She gives out a sigh.

Cute boys always spring up in her conversations whenever Aman's girlfriend pops up in our conversations. Manasi is smart and large; Aman's girlfriend wears pretty clothes and has a thin waist.

'I think you should have run faster. You would have lost a few pounds,' I poke teasingly.

'Thanks, Einstein,' she says. 'You could use a few pounds. Don't your bones hurt when you sit down? How does it feel to have, like, no flesh?'

'It feels great that I can run fast. So when a zombie apocalypse happens, you would make an easy and wholesome meal and I will not,' I answer back.

'Even in death, I will be of use,' she says, and smiles, showing all ten thousand of her teeth. 'You are teaching me JAVA later.'

I nod. The class ends and disperses, and no one takes note of us sitting at the last bench, one sketching, and the other texting a nameless friend who I am jealous of, since Manasi is my only friend, apart from Aman, whose whereabouts are presently unknown.

New Delhi Technological Institute or NDTI, is not the most brilliant or unique or reputed engineering college in and around New Delhi, but it is certainly the most conveniently located. If a capital city can be assumed to be the centre of a country, then NDTI was also literally at the centre of India, and we were at the centre of the country, sketching and texting.

The institute has four tall, red buildings, and although they are connected with passageways, they bear no resemblance to one another in terms of architecture, much like the students in the college who are like islands—disconnected, distinct and unconcerned about each other.

That my college mates are islands, or a cluster of islands, becomes clearer in the canteen, which is one of the older parts of the college, because education or not, food is food. The cool students are in the corner sharing pictures, making plans; the studious ones are sharing notes; the buff students are discussing gym routines, and there are no passageways that connect these islands of people to one another.

'You still didn't tell me, who are you texting?' I ask.

'I am not texting, I am instant messaging. It's my brother,' she says. 'The one who gifted me the phone? You should get a new phone too.'

'I don't need to instant message anyone. I'm pretty sure no one is in such a hurry to receive my messages. And my phone is fine. I can call and I can text. I don't need applications to tell me what my hair will look like or what's the weather like outside!'

'That's lame,' she responds.

I use an old Nokia, the one which was secretly made out of toughened titanium or something, built to withstand holocausts and wars. It has Snakes on it, which is my favourite game, so I am happy with my phone.

'Stop it with your new phone!' I say irritatingly as I watch Manasi distorting pictures to make thin people look fat and fat people thin. She makes herself thin but her nose grows longer in the process and I don't think I like her like that.

'Don't be jealous,' she retorts and stuffs her mouth with french fries dipped in ketchup which is suspiciously thin and watery, and pinches the screen of her phone and makes herself even thinner. 'That is perfect! That's how I want to be.'

'That's hideous,' I say.

'Jealous!' she snaps at me.

Manasi weighs ninety-three kilograms. At least that's the number she goes by, even though it has been a year since she last stepped on a weighing scale. She doesn't consider herself a foodie or a gourmet with a taste for fine food because she is quite the opposite. She just eats a lot, eats everything and eats all the time. But unlike other fat people who believe it's okay to be fat, she hates herself and on days when she hates herself the most, like today, she eats even more.

'Here he is!' I say as Aman, our only other friend in college, and the one who's cooler than us by miles, walks towards us with his trademark swagger and a half-smile, half-smirk on his face, which is gorgeous from all angles.

'What's up, dude?' he asks and stretches the 'U' in the 'dude' for a few seconds and it sounds cool, or maybe it's cool *because* he does it. Aman is too cool for his own good; he has no business hanging around with us, the real-life representation of Laurel and Hardy, except in this case, Hardy is a nineteen-year-old girl. Which reminds me that I had gifted a copy of *A*

*Fine Mess*, a pictorial book on the lives of Stan Laurel and Oliver Hardy, to Manasi on her birthday. I had thought it was a thoughtful gift but Manasi thought otherwise and said, 'I am not that fat!' She was right. Oliver Hardy was a hundred pounds heavier, though he lost one hundred and fifty pounds before his death which made him lighter than Manasi in the end. I pointed that out and she didn't talk to me for two days and I learned that girls don't like being compared to heavy, male actors.

'You just missed an important Advanced JAVA class and seeing Manasi lose weight by pinching herself on her new cell phone. Show him!' I ask her.

Manasi thrusts the screen with the thinner version of herself at Aman's face and Aman says, 'Cool!' stretching the Os till it sounds like that's the only way people should actually say the word.

'I love the phone, man,' he says and starts tapping on random applications.

'You can keep it,' Manasi says and blushes.

'That's so sweet of you, but no thanks,' he answers. He was now racing a Peugeot 500 down the streets of downtown Manhattan on Need for Speed (NFS)—only for Apple iOS—and I can so imagine him do it in real life.

'It's a gift,' I say.

'But it's mine to give away!' she snaps, her eyes icy-cold when they look at me, and marshmallow-like when they look at Aman.

'I could play this all day!' Aman says. 'But I have tennis practice. Our college team sucks and I am a part of the suckery.'

'You're awesome. I have seen you play!' Manasi counters.

'You're too kind,' he says, and just then his car crashes against the wall and the man in the car pixelates and dies. Blood splashes on the screen and the phone asks if he wants to continue. 'I can really do this all day . . .'

'Yes, you can,' Manasi says, happy to have him glued to her phone. Aman hands it back to her.

'I have Snakes on mine. You can play if you want to,' I offer Aman my phone.

'I don't want to beat your score, man. You will always be the undefeated champion of the great game of Snakes. It used to be fun though,' he says, breaks a solitary fry in two and eats it. *No wonder he's in such great shape!* Manasi can take a tip or two from him, especially since she spends so much time staring at him. Aman then asks me about the class and what all he's missed, calls me a genius at computer languages—which isn't literally true but true enough—asks me if I would teach him, and I say of course I will, while Manasi just stares at him adoringly.

'Hey, Deep. Are you still going to Hong Kong? Did your mother give you permission yet?' he asks.

'I don't need her permission to go anywhere,' I stamp my foot.

'Oh, shut up! She doesn't even let you cross the road by yourself,' Manasi interjects.

'She's just a little protective,' I say defensively.

'Little? I am surprised you don't have those CIA anklet things that help track movements. Your mom will be so happy to get you one!' she says and laughs and looks at Aman to see if he's laughing, but he is just standing there, looking handsome in his half-smirk, half-smile.

'Still a better investment than an iPhone!' I say.

'But do get us something from there, champ,' Aman says and pats my back. He often addresses me as champ, champion, genius, THE man, super-dude, and I quite like it.

'I will,' I say.

'Don't get me a book about fat people,' Manasi says.

Aman is looking away from us. A few girls from the other section pass us by and wave at him. He waves back at them and they blush and giggle. Manasi frowns. It's never pleasant to have a crush on the college's hottest guy (especially when he is already dating a slim, pretty girl). It also doesn't help that Aman is sensitive and smart, and in a weird sort of way, he is a passageway. You have to have a crush on him in order to move on.

Aman leaves for his tennis practice and Manasi starts tapping on the phone again. She is playing NFS now. We sit there for an hour, Manasi tries to better Aman's score and fails, and I read a book; we wait for the next class to start.

3

It's a big deal, believe me, but my Hong Kong Project is not being celebrated enough. Manasi is uninterested in my going because I think she will miss me, although she hasn't said it herself, and Mom's crying because her only son will be across the border, actually two borders if the aircraft flies over Nepal and into China and three if we fly over Nepal, Myanmar and China, which I would like better since I have never been on an aeroplane before. I still believe clouds are made of fluffy, soft cotton and not vapour. I would soon get to the bottom of this.

Atan Technological Services, an Indian software giant with annual revenues of over $ 7 billion, chose five first-year students from over six hundred IT and Computer Science engineering students who applied for a paid internship in one of their numerous live projects. Paid internships for students like us is like winning free tickets to a One Direction concert, it's like a bravery badge.

The woman from ATS had scanned my résumé and the ridiculous list of books I have listed as my favourites, and she asked me if I would like work in the development of a cataloguing software that ATS was developing, taking the Hong Kong Central Library as a test case.

I remember the churning in my stomach, the dizziness, the happiness that coursed through every inch of me, and I had smiled and nodded my head like a baby seal, happy and grinning from ear to ear.

'I would love to!' I had said, trying to control my excitement.

'I am not sure about the details but you might have to go to Hong Kong for a little while during the project. I will have to get back to you on this,' the woman had said.

I couldn't wait to tell my parents and when I did, Mom cried and said she would let me go only over her dead body, and Dad reminded me of Bengali pride and recounted to me the names of everyone in our family who had ever worked or works in a library. If all libraries combined to make a country, we would be the first family of that country. And I was going to add another feather in its cap.

We ate *muri ghonto* and *shorsher maachh* that day, and Mom cried some more, and then smiled because she saw a CISCO advertisement on television which welcomed us to its Human Network and the voice over informed Mom that 'libraries travel across the world', which she quickly inferred as since libraries travel across the world her son wouldn't have to. Anything to hold her nineteen-year-old son back. She was mistaken.

Today, the class is IT Infrastructure and Manasi and I don't need to concentrate because I have gone through the book, cover to cover. I love new books, course books or not, and I enjoy underlining the living hell out of course books and making little notes in my flowery handwriting on the margins.

'Hey, stud! When do you leave?' Aman asks.

'The week after next. There is still time,' I say. Aman is grinning, he's constantly grinning, and that may be because he knows he's beautiful when he's grinning. He's also playing Temple Run on Manasi's phone and his hand-eye coordination sucks, which is strange because only yesterday he won an inter-college tennis doubles trophy all by himself.

Aman would make a great hero in a Young Adult book: courteous, handsome and sensitive—a curious mix of Edward Cullen and Augustus Waters, without the canines or the cancer. I always end up associating people with characters from books. The professor is boring, he is the kind of character that dies in a Robert Ludlum book and no one misses him.

'Man! You're so lucky. Do send us pictures of all the pretty women you hang out with in Hong Kong,' he says, then realizes his folly (I have almost never dated!), and restarts his game.

'I will send you pictures of the library and the clock tower and of Disneyland,' I say and he laughs.

'I can't believe you won't be here for my birthday, dude,' he says. 'It's going to be amazing! Ritika is planning something big. She constantly asks about you and whether you would be here.'

'She doesn't even know him that well!' Manasi butts in. 'Oh, did I tell you guys? I saw this really cute guy who offered me a seat in the bus. He was looking at me, I could tell, and then I looked at him, and then I stared and then he got off the bus. I wonder if he offered me the seat or he just had to get up and I happened to be there,' she sighs.

'You should have talked to him, Manasi! You let go of way too many cute guys,' Aman says, innocently.

The professor looks at us, shoots an icy look, and goes back to drawing flowcharts on the board.

Aman tells me, 'Ritika does like you. She has like a million single friends in Miranda House. You should be there at my birthday. You will definitely meet someone.'

'I don't think anyone will be interested,' I say and not without reason. The last time I met a friend of Ritika, she had told Ritika and Aman that I was tall. She had used just one word to describe me, 'tall'. If I were in a book I would just be a tall character. Nothing more.

'Oh, c'mon! We could be going to a club and it will be so great,' he said. 'We could even get you drunk!' He winks in his charming, disarming manner, and I can see why Manasi, and whoever he meets, melts when they see him.

'I don't think that's a good idea,' I say. I don't hate clubs, but sports and dancing are my two big nemesis. My one leg is usually clueless about the other. It's like the Heisenberg Uncertainty Principle, either I know how fast they are moving or where they are moving, never both.

I have been to a club exactly twice in my entire life, and both those times I stood in a corner, playing Snakes, dressed in my loose checked shirt, my ill-fitting jeans and my chunky trekker shoes, while Aman weaved and met and hugged and danced with countless girls. Wet bodies grinded in front of me, and it looked like a perfect opportunity for contagious diseases and lice to get passed on.

Aman has been trying hard to get me interested in the idea

of drinking, but how people use digestive tracts to transform alcohol to vomit is of least interest to me.

'You can take Manasi,' I say. 'She will tear up the dance floor.'

'I can't go. I am on a diet and I will not go anywhere that will put me in the vicinity of food,' she says, even though I know she is obsessed with music and dance. She's fat, but boy can she dance! And I don't think it's the diet. Just this morning she ate a humungous sandwich from Subway.

'Oh, c'mon, Manasi! I can't go there and say my two best friends haven't come. That's not cool,' Aman says and makes a sad face, looking vulnerable; Manasi almost cries and says that she will come, and he smiles and Manasi liquefies.

'HEY! LAST SEAT! YOU THREE! GET UP!' the professor shouts and throws a chalk at us. Aman catches it millimetres away from my spectacles—cool with an emphasis on the two Os.

The three of us say, 'Us? Me? Me?' and point to ourselves.

'YES! GET UP!' We stand up and he asks, 'What are you three talking about that is so important?'

Before anyone of us can answer, and by anyone I mean Manasi and Aman because I am on the verge of tears, he shouts, 'GET OUT!'

Aman doesn't hesitate. Manasi follows him outside the class, and I stand there hoping my wet, quivering eyes, like a schoolgirl from a Manga comic, will melt the professor's heart. But he stands there, furious, his hands on his hips, and I leave the class.

'What took you so long?' Aman asks.

'I was collecting my register,' I say.

'Oh, shut up, Deep!' Manasi says to me. Then she turns to

Aman, 'He was begging the professor to let him stay. Coward!' she says disgustedly. She's Googling a new diet plan, but soon she is downloading pictures of Zayn Malik, who is one-fifth of her favourite band, One Direction, and Justin Bieber, about whom she has an unhealthy amount of information.

'I DIDN'T BEG!' I protest.

'It's good that he let us out,' Aman says. 'Ritika is about to reach here and if she invites you, you might be tempted to postpone your Hong Kong trip.'

I mumble something unintelligible. I don't like being thrown out of classes, I feel humiliated and small.

'Why is she coming here?' Manasi asks.

'She wants to meet my friends. Is that so bad?' Aman says and puts his arm around Manasi and kisses her on the cheek. Although I am a better friend, I can't do that to Manasi, but he can because he is Aman. I wish he wouldn't do that because Manasi takes it seriously. Manasi nods her head.

I spot Wasim, the cricket captain of our college, in his soiled trousers and lame cricket cap, walking towards us. He waves at Aman and as he passes by, shouts out, 'What's up! There is a crazy party tonight at Hype. You should totally come with your girlfriend, man. It would be AWESOME, dude!'

Aman nods and they do a handshake which looks like an arm-wrestling match and Wasim walks away, not looking at either Manasi or me. Despite our considerable width and length respectively, Manasi and I are like F-21 stealth aircrafts, detectable by radar, but naked to the ordinary teenage eye.

'What do you think?' Aman asks us.

'He didn't invite us,' Manasi says.

'It's like we are invisible,' I say. 'And I am pretty tall, you know. I think I am pretty hard to miss. Not that Manasi can ever hide.'

'I'm so fat that maybe he mistook me for a building or something,' Manasi says.

'Oh, c'mon, you two,' Aman says defensively. 'He doesn't know you.'

'Obviously, he doesn't. If I were you, Aman, I would never hang out with me,' I say.

'I would totally hang out with me so that I can share my food and then both the MEs will be only half as fat,' Manasi responds.

'And I will be friends with two Manasis and walk around with my arms around them like James Bond or something,' I say and pump my fist and she smiles.

Aman tells me I will have plenty of pretty women around me in Hong Kong and though I laugh, I am nervous. I have never been around people I don't know or been to places I am not familiar with, I am awkward and eye contact for me means staring at people's foreheads, but I think that's the point of travel, to see new places and meet new people and think about the lives they have lead and be them for a little while; something that books do, too.

But new people, new places scare me. Even the Delhi Metro scares me. I look at the map and it's yellow and blue and green and purple lines crossing each other. It's beautiful to look at on a map, but in real life, it's moving metal cages on wheels and concrete and real people walking very fast, bumping into each other, staring at me because I am standing in their spot.

'Here she is,' Aman points out to a girl at a distance, who's walking in our direction. Manasi's face falls. I can tell she is thinking about the imaginary cute boys in her life.

Ritika is a thin girl, a foot shorter than me. As she walks towards us, her hips sway and if great music could be seen, it would look like her hips. She has a small face which is fair and cute and proportionate and symmetrical. I feel sorry for Manasi.

'Hi, guys!' she says, in her chirpy little voice.

Aman hugs her. There is an awkward moment where I don't know whether I have to hug her or shake hands and we end up shaking hands. Manasi and Ritika smile, after which Manasi busies herself with her cell phone.

'I LOVE your college. It's so huge. I can't believe I am shocked every time I come here,' she says, as her pink handbag, which hangs from her shoulder, sways. It goes perfectly with her pink denims.

'You should come here more often,' Aman says and puts an arm around her shoulder.

'Some people don't invite me here,' she says and points towards Manasi and me, and we just smile stupidly. 'And Deep! Please do come whenever I call you. I have told so much about you to the girls. Some of them really like you.'

'Okay,' I say.

Ritika insists some more that we come to the party she's planning, and then she compliments Manasi on her hair, who blushes, because people like us, the stealth aircrafts, blush when others who are more gifted compliment us.

Aman and Ritika leave after a while. I can see they've left Manasi in a bad mood. She doesn't talk for the rest of the day and I finish the book I am reading, *The Book Thief.* It's about a girl who loses everything, starts over and then loses everything again and then . . . it's like Snakes.

4

Henner Jog was twenty-three when he wrote his first book, and it took him three more years of editing and rewriting and rewriting and editing to get the book in publishable shape. And his book is phenomenal, every sentence, every incident, every character so well thought out, that I am sure he took at least three years to write it in the first place before saying, *'Okay, maybe I can get this book published after all and blind the world with the brilliance of my words for I think it's time for me to rule the narrow passageways of libraries and every bestseller list there is to rule!'* Or maybe he just said, *'Okay, let's see what others think of my book.'* Knowing him, I think it was the latter.

This means I have a three-year head-start. Something I need badly because he's brilliant and I am, like, a tall boy who's not needed unless there's a fused light bulb.

The odds are stacked against me.

But then again, there are two million books that get published every year, probably ten times as much get written and submitted. So even while I sit in the library staring at the ceiling, watching the fan slowly rotate, wondering what triggers people to create characters and make them go through happiness, love, trauma, death and drama, trapping them in pages for other people to read and believe as if it's all happening, there is a 0.33 per cent chance that I might finish writing a book. I can take that chance to start thinking about writing a book—0.33 per cent is a lot.

There is no one who better understands this than Arindam. He signed a contract with a publishing house while he was still in his first year of English literature at Delhi University. It's been two years since the deadline has gone by; two years that he has been occupying the seat directly below my seat on the third floor of the library and he's yet to turn in his manuscript.

Arindam, himself, is like a character of a tragic book that gets turned into a bad movie. Though he is poor he had hoped life would change once he signed the contract. But after he has passed out from college, he had bills to pay and is struggling. He manages rent because he is a freelance writer for some websites and magazines but that is not enough to go by. I love him though. I love his scraggly beard, his torn bag, his ancient laptop with a few missing keys, the printed pages of his manuscript that have notes all over, and his spectacles, which hang loosely over his nose whenever he's typing. He's very short, like five feet, and is healthy for a poor guy. But he is also well read.

I was fascinated by him when my father first introduced me to him. I used to think, and I still do, that I am going to be one of the lucky few who will see a well-written, thoughtful book emerge from a brilliant writer, and see it in print and read it and appreciate its genius before everyone else, and in a small way I will be a part of the book and it will be my legacy as well.

'Hi,' I say as I approach his table. I am carrying Amit Chaudhuri's *A Strange and Sublime Address*, not only because it's written by a Bengali author, and we are proud Bengalis, and I love the book so much that I can date it, but also because I know he loves the book, and my need to impress him is as great as my desire to woo Megan Fox.

'Hey, the tall guy with the fetish for books. Come! Sit!' he says and points to the chair in front of him. I sit and smile and hope he doesn't ask me piercing questions about the book because I am not sure I get the subtexts of the books I read.

'Nice book, do you like it?' he asks.

I nod. 'How are you? How's the book going?' I ask softly, not wanting to hurt him.

'It's going great! I finally resolved the issue I was facing with the conflicting ideologies of the female protagonist. She's a bit of hypocritical slut, if you know what I mean.'

I didn't know what he means but I nod my head anyway.

'When do you finish it? And when do I get to I read it?' I ask.

'You can read it when I finish it,' he says. 'Because if I give it you now I will constantly be wondering what you think I should write. I would think of impressing you.'

*Impressing me*? I'm already way beyond impressed.

'Okay. How's work?' I ask. I really want to ask if I should start thinking about writing, but in my head it sounds like, 'Do you think I can model for women's clothes?'

'It's great. A lot of websites need a lot of things to be written for them. It's good pay,' he says and when I look at him in disbelief, he adds, 'I know what you're thinking. That why do I look like a homeless person if the websites pay me well, right?'

I don't answer.

He says, 'If I were to buy new clothes and wear them, and type on a new laptop, and live a new life, I will start feeling new and shiny, and I want the book to be old and rugged, poor and earthly, because after all, I am the book.' He lights a cigarette. Smoking is not allowed in the library, but he's special, he's a genius, and he will be the library's first home-grown writer, so he's allowed little luxuries like smoking and drinking tea on his table.

*I am the book.*

I wonder, and I wonder a lot, if it's because he said these words that they sound exotic. Would they be the same if Wasim, the cricket captain, said them? But I suspect he would add *dude* and *awesome* and *fuck* in the sentence and totally spoil it. I want to call Manasi and ask her if she feels the same when One Direction sings '*That's what makes you beautiful*'.

We talk some more about some other authors he likes, and I don't tell him about my obsession with Henner Jog, and he writes down a few books for me to read on a piece of paper; I thank him. I see the printed stack of papers next to him, crinkled at the edges, fluffed up, and I feel like having my own stack of papers printed and bound with notes on them.

'I need to work now. These website people are really far up my ass with deadlines. I will catch you around, kid,' he says and peers into his laptop screen. His spectacles slip down. I'm grateful for the chat.

I walk towards the machines of wrought-iron death, the elevators, and then to my seat and daydream about my own stack of papers imprinted with my words. Almost immediately an illusion dances in front of my eyes, I am surrounded by a wave of books that open and close and mock me for thinking

I can write, and then I argue with them, that the book is me and has nothing to do with them, and then they say they are only here to encourage me and poof! They are gone.

*I am the book.* The four words are running in my head even as I am reading *The Silver Linings Playbook*, the book whose movie made the Academy Awards jury jump up in childlike joy. Though I think the book is infinitely better, incomparable even. Maybe the book was the author and the movie was the director, maybe the author was poor and earthly and the director was new and shiny.

I spend the entire day scrawling on a piece of paper the names of all the favourite characters of the books I have read and what they are like, and I am surprised that I know more about them than I know about the people in my life.

The only one I know more about than Holden Caulfield and Augustus Waters and Tyler Durden and Mr Darcy, is myself, and as I learned today, *I am the book.*

5

Writing is HARD, and it's not with just a capital H, it's with capital ARD too, or maybe even longer words like challenging or difficult or problematic with all their alphabets in capitals, underlined and in bold. It's been a week since I decided to be amongst the 0.33 per cent people who finish writing a book every year, but all I can think of are the beautiful books I have read, of how I will let them down if I write something pathetic and unreadable. It's like performance pressure when drowning under the watchful eyes of a gaggle of coaches and parents.

I have just written half a sentence and it goes like, 'As he entered . . .' Post that I felt like death, stationary, stuck in place, and all pervasive. I felt light and disgusted, and soon, I was in a pit of inconsolable despair, clawing to get out. Staring at a blank computer screen is distressing, unromantic, and in stark contrast to feeling imprinted sheets of paper, yellowed by age and use, between your fingers.

There are 298 listed writers in the Wikipedia page under the category 'Writers who committed suicide', and like every list I'm sure it's incomplete. I shudder to think of the pressure writers are under to not write something that's hated.

I have just finished reading *Fahrenheit 451*, a novel set in the future, when houses and buildings are fireproof, and firemen don't stop fires, they start them. Their job is to burn all the books and stoke the fires that consume them, one page at a time, one story at a time.

*451 Fahrenheit* is the temperature at which the printing paper catches fire and I am that temperature. Anything that I write should catch fire and burn before anyone reads it, because reading it would destroy them.

And I hope not to destroy.

I shut down my laptop, dump my register and the solitary printed sheet with half a sentence in my bag, and storm out of the library. I have come to realize that trying to write is the single fastest path to feeling worthless.

But also, there is a little joy.

I take the Metro to college, which is conveniently located, at a ten-minute distance from Dad's library. Today we have Advanced JAVA, C++ and IT security, but I'm not worried about the classes, I'm worried about not descending down the slippery slope of depression and nihilism.

I am reading a hardback and walking towards the class, wondering if the author battled with mediocrity like I am, trying not to crash into a girl or a lamp-post, but most of all trying not to fall in my own eyes. Often deep in my thoughts, my writing is shallower than the script of Pokémon.

The book I am reading is so brilliant that I want to cry and throw it away. Instead, I just keep reading, not thinking of writing a book, and soon enough I do crash into a stupid lamp-post, the book flies out of my hand, and I am sitting on my ass, legs splayed wide open. My chest hurts, and a few girls start giggling from a distance. In all the years I have been walking, a perfect upright homo-sapiens-type walk, this is when they choose to notice me, in my brightest hour.

'Are you okay?' a voice says from behind. I turn around to see Archana, my ex-girlfriend, and she's not imaginary. Our relationship was brief but it happened.

'I'm fine,' I say. 'This lamp-post here. Stupid lamp-post, always there, never moving.'

She giggles, like she always does, and covers her mouth with her slender fingers. We were a couple in tenth grade. She was my laboratory partner in chemistry, and I remember that time in slow motion—the two of us running endlessly on a sun-kissed beach with water foaming at our ankles; we would pour silver nitrate and potassium chloride and wait for the imminent reaction, look at the bubbling of the solution and at each other, the invisible dissociation of ions, mixing together, interweaving like my fingers and hers, the precipitation of the silver chloride at the bottom the test-tube, and our fascination with it all.

We would talk about chemistry for hours at end, for I liked complex benzene rings with methyl groups hanging here and there, and she liked the thirty-something teacher who taught us the subject. Little did I know that we wouldn't last long. For, I was like an inert gas, unlikeable and uninteractive, while she was like an alkali, combustible and excitable.

As soon as we stepped into eleventh grade, she opted for Commerce and I opted for Science, and like so many long-distance relationships, ours broke down too; the corridors, the staff room between sections A and F, the water dispensers and the boys with gelled hair drinking from it. It was more than our love could handle.

I would see her on the bikes of her new friends while I still shared a cycle rickshaw with three of my tuition friends, sitting on the cushionless seat, praying it wouldn't topple over. Before long, I knew it would be over. And it was, within the first month of eleventh grade. She spent the next two years watching boys play basketball, cheering and smiling flirtatiously at them, rolling down socks to her ankles and putting on make-up while I spent it studying C++ and JAVA and mathematics.

Now she is doing BBA from my college, and today is the first time she has talked to me in three years.

'It's been so long since I last saw you,' she says.

'I see you almost every second day. Your classes are held in the building next to ours. I can see you at the window sometimes,' I respond.

'Oh.'

I didn't mean to make her uncomfortable, but it's another one of my superpowers, along with my no-writing skills.

'I'm going to the canteen. Do you want to walk together?' she asks, and I adjust my spectacles, which she understands as a 'Yes'.

'I heard about your internship and that you're going to Hong Kong,' she says. 'That's cool!'

'It's just work,' I say.

We walk in silence. I do want to talk about the time I found her licking a rather handsome boy's face in an empty classroom while she was still dating me. But I don't think it's appropriate because she did shout 'Sorry' (and that settles it) when I ran from the classroom crying and shouting, 'MOM! MOM!'

When I got home, Mom had hugged me and told me that all girls were witches who wanted to snatch her *shona* away from her. She made me *rui maachh* that day.

'Do you really see me from the window?' she asks.

I weigh the question. It could either be a flirtatious question or it could be to check whether I am a creep who watches girls sitting near the windows. I have two options:

1) Yes, I think you're still very beautiful and the fact that you broke my heart and I ate three, not two, bricks of ice cream and *rui maachh*, means nothing, so please take me back and I will lick your face too, or
2) You know I just saw you once and figured that's where you sit.

But instead I say, 'I really like your building. Do you know your building is the oldest of the four buildings of our college, and that's strange because yours is the newest course. It's ironical, and I wonder if it's intentional.' And another voice inside me shouts at me, 'YOU BIG NERD!'

'Umm . . . okay.'

Deadly silence, crushing helplessness engulfs me and I want to die. With great power comes great responsibility; my superpower of making people uncomfortable is nothing to kid around with.

'I am sorry about what happened between us,' she says. 'We never got to talk about it. You would just walk away from me whenever I tried to talk to you.'

'It doesn't matter, Archana. It was a long time ago,' I say.

'When we were together you were always into your books and never talked to me about anything else,' she says. 'I couldn't understand you a bit back in the day. I am sorry for that.'

She says it like it's a bad thing to be surrounded by books and I am not pleased. A little green Hulk pulsates inside me, puffing, nostrils flaring, fists clenching, ready to defend his territory. I stay shut.

She continues, 'I don't know why you read all those books when you can just talk to people and know so much more. It's much nicer.'

Her tone is kind and soft and apologetic, else I would have transformed into Hulk by now.

She says, 'I know a lot of people who don't read and are smart and successful and have great careers. I don't know why you had to be so into books!'

HULK SMASH! Argh!

'Books make us better people, Archana. It made me into someone who could forgive you for kissing that boy in the classroom, and it would have made you a person who wouldn't have kissed that boy in the first place. Books make you rectify the mistakes even before you make them. I am not blaming you, for I understand it was your right to find love elsewhere if you didn't find it with me. Books taught me that. It also taught me that it's important to empathize with people, because people are complex and beautiful and often irrational and hard to understand, and so are you. And my anger over that "face-eating incident" shouldn't change what I think of you as a person. It should only make me try to understand you better. When you're dead and I'm dead and the boy's dead, we can still live because we become a part of them as much as they become a part of us,' I say and I'm panting. I am a pretty stupid Hulk; Stan Lee would be ashamed.

'Boy! Okay,' she says, and flutters her eyelashes and looks at me like I have horns on my head or poop on my face, and adds, 'you should be a writer.'

'Yeah. Right.'

# 6

My parents and I stare at my suitcase. It looks small and inadequate, and we look at each other, confused. It has three shirts—none of which are world-beating—two trousers, one old jacket, five boxers, a shaving kit, my toiletries, my laptop and its charger.

'Is this enough?' Mom asks, biting her nails. 'Should I pack a few packets of Maggi? Some ready-to-eat food? Dry fruits? Anything?'

'I don't think that's necessary, Mamoni,' Dad interrupts. 'Deep, you should have spare clothes and keep more money. Also, you need to buy a pouch that you can strap around yourself—keep the passport and boarding passes and other documents there. And are you sure you checked you will get the visa on arrival?' He is checking invisible boxes in his mind.

I nod.

I stand there staring at the suitcase. All my life—boring, mundane and everyday—folded and stacked and set in it, and zipped. If one were to judge me by what my suitcase contains, I will come out as a poor guy with no fashion sense. My obituary will read: He had three hideous shirts. He also wrote a one-page, half-a-sentence novel.

It depresses me to know that I can uproot my life from one city and go to another and all I have to pack is three shirts. On the other hand, Isaac Asimov would need a gigantic trunk just to fit in the first editions of the 506 books he wrote.

'I think that's all I need,' I say and switch on the television.

'I will make a list,' Dad says and starts penning down things I have to take, buy and do, before I leave New Delhi and after I reach Hong Kong. He starts with making a list of all the numbers I can call in case of an emergency. I would rather die than call the relatives whose numbers Dad is noting down.

Mom is depressed; the zipped up suitcase a constant reminder of the empty house I will leave behind. She cries and runs to the kitchen, which today smells like all parts of heaven.

I am watching a kung fu movie on television (totally coincidental), where Jackie Chan is ripping through the streets, dancing through the crowd, jumping in and out of taxis, doing somersaults on the trams and on the trains and in subways in a city that could very well be Hong Kong, and it suddenly rings home that come tomorrow, I will be all alone in the foreign city, amidst all the madness I can see on the screen.

Suddenly, my phone rings. It's Aman.

'Hey, dude!' he shouts, the U elongated.

'Hey,' I say, trying to reflect his enthusiasm but fail.

'So, you're leaving tomorrow, right? That will be so awesome! What will you get me? And hey, don't forget to hit on the flight attendants! They're going to be so HOT. Like, really,' he says without a pause.

'Air hostesses will be the last thing on my mind. I have

never seen the insides of an aeroplane. What if I freak out while the aircraft is in the air and embarrass myself?'

'Shut up, Deep. It won't happen,' he says. 'If you're so worried, just stay strapped to your seat with a book and wear one of those adult diapers.'

I'm not sure if he is joking. Aman has more experience in locking himself in a steel cage that floats with other metal cages, vision obscured by sunlight and clouds, 35,000 feet above ground. It doesn't sound safe at all.

'Aman, there was a movie, *Snakes on a Plane*. Do you remember?' I ask, only half-joking.

'Oh, c'mon! That's science fiction, man.'

'It grossed $ 62 million, so the plot was plausible, right?' I ask.

'Harry Potter grossed a billion trillion dollars. That doesn't mean it's real or plausible, Deep!' he retorts.

*Harry Potter isn't real?*My childhood was a lie!

He continues, 'I think you're being paranoid. Everything is going to be just fine! Air travel is like the safest.'

'If you say so,' I say.

He talks about girls, nightclubs and things-to-do in Hong Kong. He knows I am going to stay locked in my hotel room counting time backwards. The thought of being away from my parents terrifies me. I'm a mumma–papa's boy.

He has read about Hong Kong on Wikipedia and is throwing facts on me, trying to get me excited about the trip.

'It's the most densely populated city in the world! Imagine being amongst so many new and interesting people,' he says.

'People scare me. You know that,' I retort.

'But it also has the most number of Rolls-Royce cars per person! Isn't that just too cool!' he continues, trying to convince me.

'It makes me feel poor.'

'Oh, c'mon. Look, it says right here, it has the most number of skyscrapers in the world. Man. If that doesn't excite you, I don't know what will,' he says, defeat creeping into his voice.

'Tall buildings make me feel small and insignificant. Also, tall buildings mean more people.'

'God help you,' he sighs.

'I'm counting on that,' I respond and he laughs, and I laugh, albeit nervously.

We disconnect the call soon after and in spite of his trying to cheer me up about the trip, I end up feeling worse. *What if I am in a place where no one understands me, I get mugged and slashed and find myself in a ditch, and I lose my passport and my three shirts?* I panic and look up the crime statistics for Hong Kong—for I think a search engine should do all the searching and we should stick to the panicking—and notice that there are fewer untoward incidents in the whole of Hong Kong in an entire year than my district has in, like, a day!

Dad completes his checklist and goes over it again, holding his spectacles over his nose bridge; his concentration, unwavering. Mom starts feeding me like this is my last meal between now and the time I come back to India.

I am bat-shit scared.

The woman from ATS calls before I leave for the airport to tell me that the trip is more of a holiday since most of the ATS colleagues I was to meet in Hong Kong had to fly out for an urgent meeting. She had mailed me an inconsequential and haphazardly put together list of things I should note about the Hong Kong Central Library. The said library looks huge in pictures, and even though the nine-floored building is dwarfed by taller ones that surround it, it stands out.

After going through my suitcase scores of times, I sit back and try not to freak out as the three of us wait in the living room waiting for the cab.

The cab arrives and Dad takes the front seat, while Mom and I huddle at the back. She holds my hands, rubs them, and occasionally cups my face and kisses it. I miss her already; I miss her kind face when she cries (she is always crying— stupid, loving Mom), I miss her hands, calloused from all the cooking and washing, I miss her incessant calls to track my whereabouts; I miss everything about her. I wish she could go too; she has never been outside India. Even though Dad hasn't ever left the border because he reads a lot, he has been to a lot of places in spirit—Mom hasn't.

'Please don't starve yourself. Try to eat. And try to find good Indian restaurants there and call me whenever you have time. I will miss you so much, shona,' she kisses me; the frequency rises with the diminishing distance between us and the airport. I'm more scared about the airport than the flying; hundreds of people rushing to catch aircrafts made of a billion little pieces welded together flying to a thousand different destinations routing through hundreds of transit cities; the complexity is insane. I have a stopover at Bangkok which only doubles my chances of not reaching Hong Kong.

The cab drops us at Terminal 3 of the gigantic Delhi airport which stands in front of us in all its modernity and glory. Cars stop, people pour out, dump their suitcases on trolleys, hug

their relatives briefly and disappear behind the retracting
doors of the airport, while I just stand there, drowning in my
mother's tears as she hangs on to me for dear life. I'm in tears
as well.

'He has to go now. It clearly says three hours before the
departure time,' Dad says, now embarrassed, but with tears in
his eyes.

'Okay,' Mom says and unwraps herself from around me
and looks away in anger.

I kiss her and she kisses me back. Dad smiles and pats my
back. Waving them goodbye is tough, trying not to trip and
fall over the trolley is tougher. I clear the security check at the
gate and wave them goodbye again as they keep watching me
from the glass door, my mom with her mouth covered with
her palms, still crying, and Dad waving at me, his hand
around Mom's shoulder.

I need them to go now. I don't want to cry because there
are girls and young kids watching.

There is a black LED display flashing in three languages the
names and timings of all the flights leaving that terminal that
day. I look for my flight's name and head towards the check-
in counter, constantly checking my pockets for the ticket and
my passport. The ground staff for the airline checks my
passport and the ticket; I ask him if I can get a window seat
and he nods. He gives me two boarding passes, one for Delhi
to Bangkok, the other for Bangkok to Hong Kong, and
wishes me luck for the flight.

The middle-aged man at the immigration counter looks at
me like I am a terrorist, a well-rehearsed doubting smirk
pasted across his face makes me shiver, but then he deems me
harmless and stamps on my virgin passport. I am ecstatic now.

I tuck my passport inside my back pocket, proceed for the security check where I place my laptop and my cell phone in a plastic bin and get myself frisked by a young security person who stamps my boarding pass. I'm on a roll!

The first thing that strikes me post-security check is the dazzling lights, even at noon, of the Duty Free area, from outlets selling chocolates to alcohol to expensive Louis Vuitton bags to watches and laptops and computers, none of which I can afford. It's cleaner and glitzier than any mall I have been to. I can see my face in the floor, and yet it's being polished again. I can't help but notice how skinny and tall I am, like a praying mantis, or a grasshopper, or their love child.

Two hours in an airport is a long time—watching people shop, scurry to their gates, and tap on their laptops can only amuse you for so long.

I walk into an open bookstore, a rather large one, that's also selling chocolates and wines, and magazines about pregnant women and dogs. I run my hands over the new hardback releases and though they seduce me like a woman with a plunging neckline, they are too expensive for my pocket.

I choose *The Mystic Masseur* by V.S. Naipaul, his first book, released when he was just twenty-three (which means I have another four years), and I start reading it. I might be sitting on the warm carpet of Indira Gandhi International Airport, but I am also in Trinidad and Tobago, living the protagonist's life in the tropical land.

Two hours aren't that long when you have the company of a good book and soon the name of my flight is announced and my pulse shoots up. Soon there will be thirty-five thousand feet between me and hard land, and jumping out will not be an option. I close the book, leave Trinidad and Tobago behind on the bookshelf, hang my backpack over my shoulder and walk towards the gate. There is a long line of people already waiting at the check-in counter. A guy from the airline tears off a part of the boarding passes and hands it back to the passengers with a smile. I stand at the end of the line, wait for my turn, and hold out my boarding pass when it's my turn.

'This is the second boarding pass, the one from Bangkok to Hong Kong. Can I have the first one please?' the Airline Guy asks me. I check and it's indeed the boarding pass from Bangkok to Hong Kong. I check my back pocket and look for the one that says Delhi to Bangkok and can't find it.

He asks to me step out of the line. My stomach churns and I panic. I flap around the pockets of my shirt and trousers, and I can't find it. I check my bag and it's not there. I am out of breath. The Airline Guy looks at me disapprovingly.

'I can't find it!' I say to him and he points to another man in a different uniform. He is the Airport Guy.

'I can't find it. I can't find the boarding pass!' I say, frantic with worry.

'When's your flight?' he asks.

'In twenty minutes,' I say, sweat trickling down my brow.

'I'm sorry. You can look for it,' he says. He contacts the Information Desk and asks them if they have found a lost boarding pass; they say no.

'What should I do now?' I ask.

He continues in a cold voice, 'There is nothing we can do. You will have to miss your flight. Can you tell me your name? I will offload your luggage.'

'*What!* I can't miss the flight. *I have to go!*' I protest. 'Can't I get a new boarding pass?'

'You can, but there is no time. You will have to go through immigration and security check all over again and that alone will take an hour,' he says. He checks my passport and tells someone to offload my luggage on his walkie-talkie. I am in complete distress. *This can't be happening!*

'Stop looking for the pass and issue a new one. He might get on the plane,' a voice from the other side says.

'But there is no time,' the guy answers.

'Try,' the woman from the other side says.

'Let's issue a new one!' I protest.

'I'm not talking to you,' the guy says. He tries to argue with the woman on the phone, clearly a senior, who asks him to get me a new boarding pass.

And just as am ready to bury my face into my palms and weep, I see a middle-aged woman in the far corner talking into a walkie-talkie. I run to her and shout, 'I really need to get on that plane! Can't we issue a new one?'

'Oh, it's you?' she says and sizes me up. 'Come with me. You kids, you lose everything. My son lost it once too.'

She walks hurriedly towards the last line of security that I crossed and I follow. And then she runs and I run after her. She ask me my name and shouts it out into her walkie-talkie and with the instruction to print a duplicate boarding pass. We wait beyond the security check line and she passes my passport to a junior to get the boarding pass stamped by immigration. She says the immigration men are hard to convince to stamp a boarding pass twice; they are old government people, cautious and lazy, and that's dangerous, she explains and I sweat some more.

'Don't worry,' she says. 'How much time do we have?'

'Five minutes,' I say.

'*Oh!*' she says and asks the person on the other side to run. I see two guys running to the immigration counter, argue with the man who doesn't seem to be in a hurry or interested in my fate, and finally cajole him into stamping it. They run back to us and hand me the boarding pass.

'Now, run!' she says. It's one minute from closing of the gate. I run and she shouts, 'Have a great trip!'

I wave as I run, and I board the plane seconds before the gates close. A smiling flight attendant points me to my seat and I blush. I am still panting from the running. After pushing my handbag under the seat in front of me because the overhead bins are closed, and I don't know how to open them, I take my seat. My legs are too long for the cramped seats. I snap close the seatbelt after I fumble with it and a fellow passenger helps me out. It's a six-year-old kid.

The aircraft starts to rumble, the beast pushes off laboriously at first, and then it moves fast, really fast. It feels unreal when it finally lifts off from the ground, tonnes of metal and people, just like that. My heart thumps so furiously that I can tell one ventricle from the other.

I look down to see the buildings get smaller, the people turn into specks and then disappear, the roads become lines, circles become points, points become pointless, till all I see are the colours red, green and blue.

The clouds surround us. They are made of cotton.

The beautiful flight attendants take turns to ask me if I need anything, and it seems unfair that they, pretty and fair and perfect, should listen to me. Every time they ask me if I need wet towels, or water, or help, I refuse, trying to be as polite as possible.

I keep staring at the spectacular view outside, and even

though there are movies on-board, which is like amazing and I hadn't believed Aman when he first told me about in-flight entertainment, for the next four hours I continue looking outside the window, my nose pressed flat against the glass, as the aircraft glides over the cotton clouds, with the sun shining at a distance, yet seeming so close—it's single-handedly the most the incredible moment of my life.

I am flying, literally.

7

The stopover at Bangkok passes by in a jiffy. I wanted to window-shop and gawk at the glittering new cameras and sunglasses, most of which cost more than my house, but I didn't want to take the risk of loitering around and losing my boarding pass again.

I am suddenly hit by homesickness and I strain my ear to hear a word or line in Hindi. Every face waiting in the line is a stranger, and I realize I will soon be surrounded by people who talk and dress differently, eat and behave differently; I will be an awkward alien.

In the aircraft, I listen closely to the safety announcements, once in Thai and once in English. It's already dark outside because, well, the earth rotates.

It's a three-hour flight and I read the magazines cover to cover, calculate how much the perfumes listed in the Duty Free magazines cost in Indian rupees, watch part of a movie I have already seen before, and then doze off with the earphones still glued to my ears. I'm woken up by a very cute flight attendant, and I sit up, my mouth still open and drooling.

'We are about to land,' she says. 'We need your seat to be upright.'

I nod, my chin wet with my drool.

*Perfect. Just perfect!*

I am cursing myself for having slept during the second flight of my entire life, as I listen to the captain's voice in my ears who informs us that we would be landing in Hong Kong soon. But when I look outside, I can only see unending darkness punctuated by little specks of light, which at first I think are reflections of the cabin's light on the glass window, but later I find they are weather bobs floating in the ocean. The flight attendant asks us to fasten our seatbelts and switch off our mobile devices, and I am still struggling to spot land. The aircraft banks left, my stomach lurches.

*There's just water beneath us. Damn it!*

And then it appears, seconds away from landing, a strip of runway, a stream of yellow neon lights separated by a wide painted road, and more yellow lights. Other runways and parked aircrafts are also visible now, but they look tiny, like parts of a Lego set, and we touchdown. It's like landing on water. As if the captain said, 'I can land on water too, but today, let's just land on the runway.' It's that close.

I sigh with relief.

After claiming my luggage, getting my passport stamped on again (Yeah, I am that good!), peeing in the urinal that is fixed a little too low for my comfort (being six feet four inches is a huge disadvantage), I exit the airport building, clutching tightly a printout with the address of the hotel I have to check in to. There is a long file of taxis, all old Toyota Camrys, in red and white, and people are hopping into them at an inconceivably rapid rate. It takes the fifty-odd people ahead of me in the line just a couple of minutes to get a cab, and when my turn comes, I dump my suitcase in the trunk and slide inside.

'Where to?' The cab driver asks in a thick Eastern accent.

'Causeway Bay, The Park Lane,' I say, thrusting the paper to his face, which he reads aloud, the same words sounding different when he says it, like a song.

'Aaaahhh! Phhark Lane, okhhay?' he asks.

'Yes.'

'Okhhay, okhhay. I thakhe you Hoowwthel Phhark Lane. Okhhay, okhhay,' he says.

He has already said 'okay' about a dozen times, as if trying to reassure me and himself that we understand each other. I ask him how much time it would take and he says about an hour. I get used to the accent pretty quickly; you just have to keep an ear out for the intonation of the vowels and guess the rest.

We leave the airport, and almost immediately I spot the city neon lights, endless rows of them. The city is like a forest, only that it has buildings, hundreds of them, in all shapes, sizes and colours.

More glowing buildings appear, the large ones now dwarfed by even larger ones, like evolution; glowing signage of corporations stick out from the top these buildings in red, blue and green. These buildings kiss the sky and light up everything around me. We cross a harbour where huge contraptions are floating on the water, probably made to lift and shift containers; the area is bathed in golden lights and the water around the harbour is a pale yellow. It's 10 p.m. and the city is a Christmas tree in a pond, water splashing right where the buildings end. It's sensational.

I pass some road signs.

Tsim Sha Tsui. Wan Chai. Kowloon. Tsuen Wan. Tsing Yi. Sheung Wan. Tai O. Lantau.

I read these names, and then read them together as fast as I can, and it feels like I am speaking their language. I smile, but the cab driver isn't pleased.

'Tall buildings!' I exclaim to distract him.

'Yes, yes. Very tall buildings. Okhhay. We build very tall buildings in Hong Kong, okhhay,' he says.

The Park Lane is in Causeway Bay and as the bell boy informs me later, I am lucky to be staying bang in the middle of an insane shopping street. I nod (No money, I want to add). As we enter the roads leading to Causeway Bay, even at this time in the night, I can spot outlets of at least a dozen luxury brands lit in brilliant golden lights; from Prada to Max Mara, from Louis Vuitton to Ermenegildo Zegna, all of them vying for my attention, and I make a mental note to come back here when I'm older and I have, like, a job. My nose is permanently pressed against the window of the taxi, amazed at the unabashed opulence. The city looks like it's Photoshopped.

My room is on the thirty-third floor, that's the highest I have ever been on foot, not otherwise. Because you know, I am a frequent flier; I just took two flights.

The room is luxurious, the little child inside me is excited and I start looking through the guides to Hong Kong, the food menu which is extensive and long, the little bottles of shampoo and moisturizer, and the bathtub, which I will have to double over to fit inside. I don't think it will be comfortable for me to lie in a bubble bath with candles lit around me, my hairless bony legs sticking out.

I call the front desk nervously, not sure if they would understand me, and because I am not good with new people.

'I'm calling from room number 332. Can I make a call to India? How much will it be?' I ask.

'Your company will pay for it,' he says, his voice irritatingly polite, and then explains how to make a call, and I thank him. He says 'okay' about five times during the conversation. It's like Hong Kong's national word!

I call on my father's cell phone.

'Deep! Deep!' my mom shouts. 'Is that you?'

'Yes, I just checked in,' I answer. 'It's a beautiful hotel. I like it. It's like Uncle Akro's house in Mumbai. It's so clean and big! There are no tubelights though. It's all yellow in here.'

'Did you eat something on the way?' she asks. 'Did you meet anyone from the office?'

'I ate a sandwich. And I think I will meet them tomorrow,' I say. I am not sure if Mom's crying or really, really happy because she sounds the same in both these cases. I start feeling homesick. She hands over the phone to Dad. He asks if I will be available on this number and I say yes. We disconnect the call.

It's already eleven. After a hot shower, I change into my night clothes and slip inside the cosy covers. The mattress is soft and promptly swallows me up. The curtains are drawn apart and at a distance, I see a brown building I remember from the pictures, the Hong Kong Central Library. Standing in the midst of soaring structures of steel and glass, all of which are taller than anything I have ever seen in my life, the library looks enchanting, almost magical, like Hogwarts, like a place where wizards realize their true potential.

I am woken up at nine next morning by the incessant ringing of the landline. It's Sameer from ATS, Hong Kong. He tells me that he is leaving for the US for a week and I should mail him if I need anything, and that he expects me follow the mail I received from them in India. He disconnects the call when the woman in the background makes an announcement to switch off all mobile devices. Mobile devices interfere with the aircrafts' communication systems. Yes, I know that because I am a frequent flier.

The list is a sham. It's NOTHING. The mail says they want me to understand the two cataloguing classifications, both of which I know since I read about them on the Internet, and see how it's applied in the Hong Kong Central Library. I'm panicking because I can't be doing nothing in this city I don't know anything about; I had planned to either hide in the office, or in my hotel room. I have always been wary about how these huge corporations work; so inefficient.

The room is awfully quiet, beautiful but quiet.

The Internet is incredibly fast, and I check for directions to the Hong Kong Central Library (HKCL). Though I can see it from my hotel window, I want to be sure. After marking the route on the map of Hong Kong they gave me at the front desk, I take a shower, lock my passport and money in the safe in my room and leave the hotel. I am hungry, but I don't know what to do about it. I don't want to start this trip by eating something I can't a) understand and b) digest.

I stand with the map in my hand, trying to make out east from west. I am also frequently distracted by the avalanche of people walking on the pavements, their strides swift and determined, their clothes impeccable, their hair smooth and gorgeous and their skins reflecting the yellow, fresh honey like sunlight.

The weather is pleasant and I start to walk towards the library, making sure it doesn't run out of my line of sight. Suddenly, I have melted into the crowd. Next to me are children in prams, kids jumping in bright yellow tracksuits, girls in shorts and dresses, women in suits tapping on their phones, moms and dads, college students—but no one is cutting or bumping into each other. It's chaos, but it's eerily organized.

The sky looks like a shopping magazine; the LED lights on the signboards that hang overhead the entire road are already glowing red and blue. Just hanging over my head are two signboards that start from the opposite sides of the road and meet midway, one selling Outback Steak, promising to send me back to the Texan lifestyle, the other selling Authentic Japanese Cuisine. It's the city of signboards and bright lights.

The roads that run past the pavements are narrow, but the traffic moves swiftly, like a snake, halting at red lights, and then accelerating ferociously as it turns green. Unlike India, pedestrians have the first right on the roads, and cars stop dead on their tracks if they see people crossing the road even when the lights are green. I almost died twice.

The bigger the vehicle, the more humbly it rolls. The

gigantic double-decker buses, pasted from headlight to tail-light with colourful advertisements selling international fashion brands to cell phones to opera and museum tickets, are menacing, but the drivers are smiling.

In the past ten minutes, I have been scared by the buses that thunder past me, turning precisely where they should, like a mammoth with a cheetah's precision. I couldn't see the tops of some of the skyscrapers without toppling over; and I have fallen in love with the women with honey skin, brown hair and a purposeful sense of dressing. But I miss home.

There are four passageways that lead to HKCL and I take the one which no one's taking, the stairs. There is a fountain in front of the library and kids are taking pictures of themselves flashing peace signs, arms around each other. The handlebar of the gate that leads me inside the library has a notification over it: This handle is disinfected six times a day.

The library has eight floors that are open to the public. Eight floors, I say to myself. It's nothing like Dad's library; this one has computers, is carpeted, has pillars shinier than mirrors, escalators and multiple issuing desks. I am Alice, and this is my wonderland!

There is pin-drop silence.

I take the escalator to the first floor, which is the children's library, and it's filled with books in Chinese and Korean and English, and everything around me is miniature. Little computers, little desks, little wooden chairs, and on them are little kids with headphones bigger than their faces wrapped around their ears; they are cuter than the word cute itself.

I feel like a giant intruding their space.

There is a playroom with a plastic tree and plastic-tree-issuing table and small kids with round faces are jumping around as delighted parents watch. There are more disinfectant stations; they make me feel dirty.

The next floor has the adult lending library, which houses racks upon racks of books about literature, history, sciences, architecture etc. It's like my Dad's library on steroids. I put my laptop bag on a table, deciding that I would savour the library a floor at a time, one layer at a time.

It takes me three hours to cover three racks of books aptly named 'Oversized English Books'. They range from *History of the World* to *History of Hong Kong* to sports and politics. There is even an oversized version of *The Catcher in the Rye*. It reminds me of the first time I read it, it reminds me of home, of Dad, and of Mom.

Holden Caulfield, the seventeen-year-old from *The Catcher in the Rye*, crowds my mind, and I start to feel like him, alone in the city where no one's listening, only slightly happy and mostly distraught, missing his family. But he whines and I am not whining, for I am imagining myself not moving out of this library for a really long time.

I spend the next six hours at the library.

8

If the elevators in Dad's library are Indian-made mid-level sedans, the elevators at my hotel are like racetrack Ferraris with nitrous oxide cylinders. It only takes me seconds to reach the thirty-third floor from the ground-floor lobby.

So far I have only eaten a sandwich in the last twelve hours, and even though my sensory organs are mauled by a million delightful smells and sights of food from countries I don't even know the capitals of, I am anxious about ordering the wrong thing. Hotel food can be trusted, I say to myself, more so because the guy at the front desk understood me earlier.

The lift lobby has eight elevators and a lot of mirrors. I presume people like to look their best before they board a lift.

Ting!

A lift farthest to my right opens and I run before it snaps close. I press the button to my floor and start counting seconds. I am on my fifth second (seconds go slower when you count) when I see the reflection of the girl behind me on the lift's door. She's leaning on the mirror, standing there nonchalantly like she's not the most beautiful girl ever to walk the face of earth.

She's staring straight ahead. Her hair, brown and golden and with big, wavy curls, falling all over face, reaches down to her shoulders. I am not sure where she's from, because she's too fair, and her eyes are a curious shade of green and blue, but her earrings look Indianish and the tattoo on her hand is in Devanagari script. She's dressed like a hippy—harem pants and a heavily embroidered kurti, beads wrapped around her wrist, lots of them. Maybe she went to India for spiritual purposes after having too much of the Black Eyed Peas or something.

She's leaning back but I can make out she's not tall, around five feet three inches I would reckon. I am hoping she doesn't spot me looking at her reflection. In her presence, I feel rather inadequate and insufficient. I also feel kind of breathless.

The seconds slow down further.

10. 11. 12. 13.

The button of my floor is still glowing. I notice that it's the only one glowing on the entire panel. *She is also going to my floor!* Suddenly, I am a mush, a pile of nerves and muscles, and I am sweating. I get my shit together and concentrate on exiting the lift without tripping over anything and getting my face busted open.

30. 31. 32. 33. Ting!

The lift doors open and I walk out, forcing myself not to look back. I hear the shuffling of feet behind me, all the way to my room, and after a few seconds, I can hear another door unlock and then lock again. She's close by, and that gets my heart into a tizzy.

Back in the room, I call up Mom again and she asks me if I have eaten anything and makes a major fuss when I tell her the truth. Dad asks me to go down and have something right away. It's slightly cold, so I put on a jacket. I'm not thinking of the girl, but the awareness that she's in a room nearby makes me uncomfortable. *The bluish green eyes!*

I'm back in the lift and I'm going down to the cafe of the hotel. It's seven and there are already a few people there, eating and talking. There is large kitchen bang in the middle of the restaurant and you can see chefs in their towering white hats cooking in open flames, and though everything looks like it's burning, it smells like a feast. I take a seat close to the window, away from everyone else and watch the cars zip past on the flyover which is only about four arms away from me.

I order a ramen soup, because it has chicken and eggs and noodles in it and I can almost eat the picture printed on the menu. I start reading *Maharani* by Ruskin Bond, the unchallenged maharaja of short stories; but this is a novella which charts the life of a prodigal yet charming queen, and her relationship with Ruskin Bond. It retains the charm of his magical short stories that I have grown up reading. Maharajas getting nibbled to the bones by pet rats, philanderer drivers shot in their heads while still entwined with queens in amorous embraces, impotent kings and sex-starved queens, it's all there.

I am reading this because I don't want to be seen, or talked to, and books have always been my friend when I have wanted that. The bowl of soup and ramen and chicken arrives, with two chopsticks by its side, and a soup spoon—no forks.

After a careful examination of the people sitting around me, I hold the chopsticks and snap them like the claws of a crab as I try to grab hold of a bunch of noodles. My grip loosens and I drop the chopsticks into the bowl. The second and third attempts yield the same result. A three-year-old sitting at a table to my left is using chopsticks like Samurai swords, very disheartening.

I am really hungry now, almost salivating like a rabid dog into the bowl. Finally on my fourth attempt I manage to wrap around my chopstick, a never-ending noodle and somehow slurp at it long enough for it to reach inside my mouth. I chomp on a piece of chicken, and momentarily, I am in heaven.

I hear someone giggling. Damn it. So much for being invisible.

My eyes dart from left to right, scanning the place like an MI6 agent, looking for the one who giggled, so that I could eventually, well, do nothing with that information.

And then I see her sitting with earphones dug deep into her ears, three tables away from me, looking straight ahead and not at me, but still giggling. She has a coffee cup in front of her, which she takes sips from once in a while, without looking at it.

I get back to my reading and finish the last few pages of the book. I am getting better at using chopsticks, snapping them like a blindfolded ninja catching pieces of chicken mid-air. After I am done, the waiter gets me the bill and I sign it. The girl is still sitting there bobbing her head to the music, occasionally sipping her coffee, looking in no specific direction. There is a constant smile on her face, like Mona Lisa's, there for an unknown purpose, timeless, beautiful.

The book ends, but I don't want to leave the cafe, so I order a coffee as well. It arrives and I start reading the newspaper that's on my table, stealing glances at the girl from time to time. Next thing I know, she's gone. I curse myself for getting distracted by an article in the newspaper which wasn't even interesting. I ask for the bill again, sign it and run towards the lobby. People are looking. I always think people are looking, even when I know they are not.

I find her standing in the lift lobby. The lift reaches the ground floor and I am still running to get there. Just before the golden gates close, I slip my hand in and the doors retract. She's leaning against the back of the lift; the light on the thirty-third floor button is glowing.

'Sorry,' I mutter.

'It's okay,' she says. I look at her in the reflection again. Oh. My. God. Those. Eyes.

12. 13. 14. 15. The lift's moving too fast.

I am staring at her on the polished doors of the elevator. Her lips move, she says, still without looking at me, 'Are you from Kolkata?' Her voice is smooth, without kinks, like whisky. I have never had any but I hear it's smooth.

'Huh?' I look at her. 'From Delhi. But I am a Bengali. How do you know?'

She turns her face towards me, not exactly towards me and says, 'You smell like Kolkata.'

I am thinking stale fish and dirty sea, unwashed clothes and dingy lanes, and I ask, 'How?'

'You smell old,' she answers and looks straight ahead.

33.

I walk ahead of her as she bides her time. Not looking back, I walk to my room, wait for the door of her room to be unlocked and locked again, and only then do I enter the room, fall flat on the bed and think about her wavy hair, her whisky voice and the accent, slightly Indian, slightly alien. I doze off on the bed too large for me thinking about her. *I smell old.*

It's only 9 p.m. when I wake up. I am hungry again, I guess because I have nothing else to do. Gathering up the shreds of courage and self-respect that I am left with, I fire up my laptop and close my eyes and wait for the words to come to me. Zilch.

There are only three things that come to my mind. 1. It's going to be predominantly autobiographical and 2. A part of it is going to be a love story, so that's going to be fictional and 3. I am already contradicting the points I am sure about and 4. I am never going to write the book and 5. I said I had only three things in my mind . . .

Three hours of staring at a blank screen yields one paragraph, no more, no less, about a hundred words. I read these words repeatedly, and though it isn't brilliant, world-changing, metaphor-laden prose, they are still the first few sentences written by me:

*As he entered the hotel, luxurious and opulent beyond his zaniest dreams, he felt privileged, spoilt, and even lucky. More so when he found himself next to a girl who was beautiful, fair and proportionate, like a goddess and the figures in Da Vinci's sketches. He wanted to make sure it wasn't one of his open-eyed dreams. They were on the elevator to the top of the hotel, and he could see them, the girl and him, riding together into the sun, like the elevator of the chocolate factory that broke right through the building and floated into the yellowness, the yellowness of the sun, the yellowness of Hong Kong. Aha! Hong Kong.*

I read and re-read my sentences, and then I sleep like a child.

9

The phone's ringing again. It's Sameer from ATS, Hong Kong, but he's calling from the US. Life's fancy like that; sitting in a hotel room in Hong Kong, I get calls on the landline from a senior who works in Hong Kong but is stationed in the US for a meeting. Am I cool or what!

'Hi! I hope you're having a great time in Hong Kong. I'm sorry I couldn't be there. But you need to go to the office once. Ritik, my colleague, will see you there. He will tell you what sort of work we do at ATS, Hong Kong. You can add that in your project report,' he says in a monotone. His voice is so boring, it's good he's a million miles away.

'Sure, sir,' I say.

'Fine. Do what he asks you to do,' he says and disconnects the call.

Google Maps places the office fifteen minutes away from where I'm staying. The thought of using public transport petrifies me. It's already eleven. I am not a heavy sleeper and I never stay in bed after seven, but there's something about the mattress, it's as if it's made of roses and sleeping pills.

The bathtub invites me, but I'm the praying mantis, with

long legs and shit, and I'm a young man so I shower instead. I pick the best shirt of the three, moisturize my face till it's slick like butter paper, lock my room·and head out. I walk slowly, deliberately, hoping to bump into her again, but I'm alone in the lift. So alone.

After confirming the address at the front desk, I leave the hotel, where every employee smiles at me, their eyes disappearing in happiness and crinkles of their skin. They make me feel wanted and that's new. The subway station is a ten-minute walk. The roads are still crowded with people, dressed far better than I am.

As I get into the subway, I notice that the entire population is on touch devices, tabs and iPhones and iPods, and when I say *entire*, I mean the word literally. A series of long, winding escalators take me down to the Customer Service window where I buy an all-day pass for tourists, just in case I feel brave enough to act like one. The Metro isn't much different from the one I board in India. It's as crowded, just that here I don't feel molested and like I am being smashed to a pulp.

The building isn't hard to find. It's a hundred-floor building, that's ninety-eight floors more than my apartment building in Delhi. The ATS office is on the thirty-fourth, thirty-fifth and thirty-sixth floors of the building, and I set a new record. Yes!

Ritik is waiting for me near the reception. He's a short balding guy, much like R.K. Narayan's common man in a shiny, fitted suit. He's fit though, and he breaks out into a big smile when he sees me, and then he crushes my hand in a firm handshake and says, 'Welcome to ATS, Deep. You're so tall!'

'Thank you,' I say. For years I have been looking for a repartee to when people call me tall but I have not come up with one yet. So for now, I just keep staring at the top of his head listlessly.

'Let me show you around the office. Have you been to our office in Bangalore?' he asks and I shake my head. 'It's pretty much the same, but we have a lot of people from Hong Kong working here.'

I nod. He shows me around the three floors of the office, walking swiftly between cubicles, waving to people who are peering into fancy computers with two screens. The conference rooms are occupied, the people are sharply dressed. And contrary to what I had expected, the Indian representation here is pretty low.

'So what do you want to do? I heard you have a mail with instructions to go by? Show me,' he says and points to the laptop on his desk. It's an ASUS gaming laptop with a keyboard whose sides are glowing red. Attached to it are sparkly Skull Candy headphones. Ritik's not as dead sexy as Aman, but he's definitely cool.

'Print it out. I don't want to stare at a screen for a minute longer than I have to. I don't want to be blind and spectacles kill my swag, man,' he says. I hand over the printout to him, he reads it, looks at me and starts to laugh. 'This is a joke, man, no offence to whoever assigned this to you. Let me tell you something. I will find you a computer and send you a demo of the cataloguing software we have developed here. You can test it out. It won't take more than an hour or two. Tell me if you can find ways to improve it. I already have a report on the software. I will mail it to you and you can make some changes and submit it. No biggie.'

'Sure,' I say.

'Don't sound so nervous, man! It's no big deal. To let you in on a secret, the software is fucked up right now. And if you get bored of it, you're free to download games from the LAN and try out a few rounds of Counter Strike,' he chuckles. 'I was against the whole internship idea, but they just don't listen. The HR department wants to catch talent young. So just relax and enjoy your holiday.'

'Fine, sir.'

'And maybe we can go out in the evening? I will get my wife along. Sounds like a plan?'

I want to say I–don't–go–out–in–the–evening–and–it–sounds–like–a–disaster but I say, 'Okay.'

'If you need to eat, there's a cafeteria down the hall. Everything's on the house!' he says and pats my back. 'And hey, I want to see you at at the club cluster near Central. Just ask anyone. They will tell you where it is. Sharp at nine.' He winks.

He finds me a laptop and then leaves. I test out the cataloguing software demo. It's crude and still at the development stages. I make a list of my observations and mail it to Ritik who asks me to slow–down–in–life–man–and–play–some–Counter–Strike.

Instead, I download the document with the first paragraph I have ever written. I brace myself for a few hours of excruciating depression as I start typing again.

I spend another afternoon without eating, but this time it's because I am writing and re-writing furiously—my brain's a furnace and it feels like it is going to explode. I have heard somewhere, 'The art of writing is rewriting.' It rings true now. I have managed another paragraph and with this I have the license to read my words in print. I hit Crtl + P and wait for words to materialize on paper.

I spend the entire time on my way back, from the subway to my hotel, reading the words on the paper. Soon they lose meaning and disinterest me, and I think of twenty different things I can add to the text, and it all seems wrong, but they are still my words, my key to immortality.

'*As he entered the hotel, luxurious and opulent beyond his zaniest dreams, he felt privileged, spoilt, and even lucky. More so when he found himself next to a girl who was beautiful, fair and proportionate, like a goddess and the figures in Da Vinci's sketches. He wanted to make sure it wasn't one of his open-eyed dreams. They were on the elevator to the top of the hotel, and he could see them, the girl and him, riding together into the sun, like the elevator of the chocolate factory that broke right through the building and floated into the yellowness, the yellowness of the sun, the yellowness of Hong Kong. Aha! Hong Kong.*

*The little luxuries of the tiny shampoo bottles notwithstanding, he still thought of the girl in the lift, fair and radiant, with a strange determination in her eyes, a musician's wardrobe, or a hippy's, he couldn't tell. He couldn't help but think of how she had walked away from him, like life itself, and how he was left robbed of her, and of life, when she disappeared into her room. He waited in the lobby, walked around in circles, waiting for her to come out and step into the same lift with him, again, but she didn't. Tired, he went to his room and slept, memories from earlier that day clouding his mind.*'

The elevator is still empty.

10

I wake up to the ringing of the alarm.

My bed seems extremely inviting as I struggle to open my eyes. I notice a tiny red light flashing on the landline. I reach out to press the play button and hear a frantic Ritik over the din of men and women and dub step, 'NINE P.M. THERE IS AN OUTLET THAT SELLS WRAPS AND STUFF. IT'S RIGHT WHERE THE CLUBS END. NINE, NINE OKAY! YEAHHH!'

I look up the location on Google and the results unsettle me. It's a street known for its clubs and nightlife; clearly not my thing.

The phone starts to ring just then.

'Maa?'

'Deep? Where have you been? I called you in the morning, shona, and no one picked up. Your father and I have been worried sick. Are you okay? Why didn't you call earlier?' she asks, as if I have been missing for days.

'I'm okay. I went to the office. It's very nice. I might go out tonight with colleagues. They asked me and I couldn't say no.'

'What? But it must be after six there!' she exclaimed. My curfew in New Delhi is 6 p.m. and after 6 in the evening, Dad and I were supposed be within one arm's distance of my mom, no exceptions. We didn't dare to cross her.

'It's eight here.'

'EIGHT! *Ishhhhhh*. No, shona, you're not going anywhere. You are alone in that city and we don't know anyone there. You don't even have a phone. You're not going, promise me, promise me, you'll not go.'

'I will try.'

I start talking about food and she gets distracted. I tell her about the allowance I had learned about earlier and ask her if she needs anything from Hong Kong. She tells me to spend it on myself, but I already have my eyes fixed on a handbag I'm sure she will like. It's no Coco Chanel, but it's definitely better than the ancient, tattered jute bag she uses.

I ask if I can talk to Dad because if there is an authority on how to conduct oneself in public gatherings it's him (he's the deputy chairman of our colony's Durga Puja), but he's cutting vegetables and his hands are dirty. It seems like ages since I have been home; I have even started missing helping out in the kitchen. I don't like doing the dishes, but I'm a mutant when it comes to cutting vegetables into thin slices.

I disconnect the call.

The shirt issue strikes me again! I used my best shirt this morning, so I pick the second best hoping Ritik and his wife would be too drunk to notice the shirt. Or me. I need to buy a shirt soon—I make a mental note.

It's 8.30 in the evening but it's still day in Hong Kong. The sky is cloaked with buildings and signboards, and they are awash with lights. The sun never sets here. The subway is as crowded as it was in the morning, and if it is possible, the people are even better dressed than in the morning.

The clubbing district is a stone's throw away from the subway station. I take a taxi and look out of the window to see men and women, dressed in suits and Little Black Dresses (which I think are Too Little), disappearing into clubs. I am positive I would be mistaken for a cleaner and handed a mop.

I walk around with a sense of urgency, trying to look for a familiar face but I'm easily distracted by the flashing lights of the packed clubs on both sides of the streets, and before I know it, I have walked twice around the two magical streets that comprise the district. I'm again reminded of what Aman had said about Hong Kong being the most densely populated urban centre, because everyone seemed to have descended to this street of frolic and unending parties. Back to my senses, I start looking for Ritik again; unknown people with drinks in their hands raise their glasses and wish me the best night ahead as I pass them.

I'm so out of place.

OUTLET THAT SELLS WRAPS AND STUFF isn't hard to find. It's right where the street starts and I don't know how I missed it. The streets are my kryptonite: bars with women, lots of women! I'm still like the eighth grader who doesn't hate girls any more, instead likes them, but they are so new to him that it's frightening.

'HEY! You made it! What up?' he shouts. I can hear no music, but he's still shouting. He's definitely, positively drunk.

'Yes. It wasn't hard to find,' I say, wriggling out of his embrace.

'This is my wonderful wife, Connie! And this is Deep, the brilliant intern,' he says. A delightfully short woman waves at me. 'Isn't she just beautiful? Look how cute she is!' He kisses her and she curls up into a shy ball.

'He's really drunk. Hi! I'm Corinna Cheung,' she smiles, her eyes cute like a bug's, disappearing into the crinkles of her skin. We shake hands. Then she turns away from me and joins her group of women. They all start talking loudly in what could be Korean, Chinese, or Vietnamese.

'How do you like it?' Ritik asks, grinning widely. He's still in his office clothes; his eyes are bloodshot and he's looking at his wife. 'If it weren't for her, I would have left this city long back. But now, "Woàitâ, woàizhèzuòchéngshì." (I love her and I love this city.)'

'Was that Chinese?' I ask, shocked. He laughs.

'Yes, it is. I didn't want to lose out on a single word she says.' He's still looking at her. 'And man, the first time I heard her talk, it was like music, and I felt so bad I didn't know what she was saying. So I took classes and now I know exactly what her relatives say about me and let me tell you, they love me like crazy! I don't blame them for that!' He laughs again.

'Woàini!' (I love you) he shouts at Connie and Connie smiles and says, 'He's too drunk.'

'I will just be back. Let me show Deep around. And I'm not nowhere near drunk!'

'That's a double negative.'

He frowns. 'Oh, so now you're going to be all Shakespeare with me.'

'Geoffrey Chaucer,' I correct him.

'Now who's that?'

Before I can tell him that he's, like, only the father of English grammar he tells me I should get a girlfriend.

'You like it? You like it?' He asks with a childlike enthusiasm as he takes me around the two streets again. We walk gingerly through the streets, which are now teeming with even more people, all of them about my age but infinitely better-looking, many of them screaming and dancing like the world is ending in a couple of hours. Crowds have spilled over from the clubs and bars onto the streets. I spot just like in the movies, groups of boys and girls standing around in a circle, gasping and cheering a solitary dancer's busting moves.

It looks like I have stepped onto the sets of a *Step Up* sequel. Everyone's a phenomenal dancer, and everyone's having a great time.

'Now let's get you bent, homeboy.'

Before I can ask him what 'bent' means and devise excuses to keep myself away from the drinking or the dancing, he says, 'Bent means drunk!'

# 11

'This is the best!' Ritik pushes a flaming shot at my face. I think he has just burned one of my eyebrows. The group of girls with Connie, his Chinese wife, are wreaking havoc on the dance floor.

'I can't drink it.'

'WHAT?'

'I SAID I CAN'T DRINK IT, RITIK!' Before I can finish the sentence he forcibly pours the drink down my throat and it burns wherever it touches as it goes down, which is everywhere.

'That's disgusting!'

'Welcome to Hong Kong!' He laughs throatily.

And then Connie walks towards us with her legion of genetically engineered dancer friends. 'You are not drinking? Come drink!' And as if on cue they start chanting, 'Drink! Drink! Drink!'

And then I feel myself dissolving in the flaming shots of Whatever the Heck It Is.

Half an hour later, I am pretty bent, like, really bent. I remember myself—flailing legs trying to kill someone, and Connie laughing and telling me that I dance like a fish out of water, that I flap my limbs like a headless chicken.

Being 'bent' is kind of like being victorious, it's powerful and liberating, and yet it's lonely, like it's only you who can feel the utter joy of flying, but you're flying alone even in a crowd and there are no cotton clouds.

'You smell weird.'

I am banging my head on the bar table because the world's spinning like a goddamn carousel. I remember Ritik helping me up on a bar stool after my dance moves were deemed a threat to public safety in general. I also remember having complete conversations, though I don't remember a word of what I said, with an American student studying dentistry, a German pole vaulter on vacation, wildlife photographers from Australia, and a group of bubbly honeymooners from India. That's the most culturally diverse experience I had ever had in my life, even though I was, like, totally smashed.

The bartender is serving drinks at a frantic pace; there is literally no place to stand. It's dark with flashy lights.

Connie, her friends and Ritik are still dancing. Ritik is as bad a dancer as I am. He's crossing his hands, flashing gang signs, and from a distance it would seem like he's eve teasing his own wife.

'You smell old.'

I look up because I feel it's addressed to me. 'Huh?' That's my best response because I am like why-is-a-girl-talking-to-me.

'You're the guy from the lift, aren't you?' She laughs. She is definitely the girl from the lift, the girl from the first two paragraphs from my book, the pocket-sized hippy. She is sitting on the bar stool next to me, legs swinging, smiling to herself.

'Yes,' I blurt. My throat closed up. Our legs are touching under the bar table and I am frightfully aware of it. Between me and my speech hangs her beautiful face like a cloak, blocking my words.

She sips her coffee. She doesn't look at me; I don't blame her, I don't look like anything worth seeing, and I smell old. She smells like hotel room shampoo and strawberries and fresh lilies like she does. She's staring at the neon-lit sign behind the bartender that screams in yellow and red: FREE DRINKS FOR LADIES.

'Is your coffee nice?' I ask.

She nods, she has a coffee moustache over her full lips that are like little pink dew drops, and she's still not looking at me. 'I didn't know what else to order. But it's almost the best coffee I have ever had.'

'Who are you here with?'

'Dad.'

'Oh.'

Aman says I'm funny and if that's the case, this is the right time to bring it on, bring it on like the freaking tsunami, but I am silent like a faulty water sprinkler.

'I drank something which was on fire. It was terrible,' I say.

'Drinking is lame. Coffee is better. Although my dad differs. He's quite the authority on alcohol. I have heard we have a huge bar at our house in India.' She laughs, and it's like drunken birds chirping, melodious and wonderfully out of tune.

'What do you do?' I ask, putting the water sprinkler on.

'I play a few instruments, though I'm not very good at it. Also, I'm blind.' She sips her coffee.

'You're *what*?' I ask, not sure if I heard her right and to confirm that it is not just an excuse she uses to ward off strangers.

She licks her lips. 'I'm blind. I have Leber's congenital amaurosis. I feel so good about myself whenever I can pronounce it correctly. It's such a big word.'

'I know bigger words,' I say. 'Like Pneumono-ultra-microscopic-silico-volcano-coniosis. It's the longest word in the English dictionary.'

'That's impressive!' she beams.

'Are you really blind?' I asked, still unsure, and trying to make sense of the missing eye contact between us, which is fine because I'm not a big fan of making eye contact. 'You can't see anything?'

'It's called visually impaired.'

'I'm sorry. I didn't—'

Her laugh is like drunken birds' laugh—chaotic and lovely. 'It's okay. I don't mind.'

'But your eyes look fine.'

'It's some problem with the nerve. That's what the doctors tell me.' She turns to me, but not really. She's looking over my shoulder, like she has a squint or something.

'I'm sorry.'

'You don't have to be!' she laughs again and it's gorgeous and I want her to stop doing it.

'You really can't see anything?'

'I see blurry figures. I can make out if it's night or day, but other than that, all I see is a mixture of colours, like a kids' painting, everything overlaps and smudges. It sort of sucks.'

'Then how do——?'

'I used to have a guide dog but he got run over. Now, I have my dad and a stick. I miss my dog though. He always smelled so terrible.'

'Is that why you could smell me? Like you have developed a supernose?'

She chuckles. 'Unfortunately, I haven't developed superears or supernose as a side effect. I must be the worst blind person ever.' She's still looking over my shoulder. 'I last saw clearly when I was five.'

'I read a book once by Tom Sullivan. He's a blind author and——'

She interrupts and she looks pissed. Her blind eyes are angry. 'Dad doesn't let me read books about blindness or by blind authors. He feels they will make me feel bad about myself.'

'I was just——'

'Though I read, or rather, I heard, *The Country of the Blind*, by H.G. Wells. It was so interesting!' she gushes, her eyes lighting up. Anyone would guess that her eyes—an extension of her face, beautiful and expressive—still work.

'The guy who wrote *The War of the Worlds*, the first superstar of sci-fi fiction! He was a genius,' I say, excitedly.

'I have heard.'

'Did you watch the movie *The War of the Worlds* as well? The book is so much better!'

'I can't see.'

'Oh, right. I'm sorry.'

# 12

Her eyes are constantly darting around us, not looking anywhere, but everywhere.

'Do you see my dad around?' she asks.

I look around. 'Is your dad in his early twenties and wears skinny red denims?' I ask cheekily.

'I wouldn't know, but I don't think so. Red is not really his colour,' she says. 'He's in mid-forties, really, really tall and sports a crew cut.'

I look around but I can only see different shades of denims. It takes me two 360-degree scans to spot the only mid-forties guy around. He's chatting up the bouncer, and he's handsome, like movie-star handsome. His arms are bulging out of his T-shirt, the nerves of his biceps are visible under his skin.

'Is your dad a fitness model?'

'Oh, you see him? He's here, right?' She breathes and smiles to herself. 'He used to be a pilot in the Indian Air Force. Now, he's a consultant.'

'Consultant to swimwear models? I don't think men in their mid-forties are allowed to be that muscular. It's against the law or something.'

'Oh, don't be mean! He's a consultant for a company that makes lightweight aircraft.'

'Fancy!' I say. 'Oh shit! I think your dad is looking at me.'

'He wouldn't mind. He forced me to come to this club.'

'Forced? Why?'

'He wants me to be a teenager and do all teenager type things and not miss out on anything. I don't think he likes me as I am. He expects me to struggle with adolescent issues too,' she laughs.

'And you have no adolescent issues?'

'Blindness takes up a lot of my time,' she says with a defeated smile.

'Your dad is still looking. He's really muscular,' I say, a bit unnerved.

She doesn't give me a direct response, 'People tell me he has a disarming smile. Is he smiling?'

She finishes her coffee and the bartender notices immediately and asks if she needs a refill. She shakes her head and the bartender smiles; I think it's the first time I have seen him do so. She takes out a ten–dollar bill from her pocket but the bartender refuses it. He says, 'It's on the house! For the beautiful birthday girl!'

'Birthday? It's your birthday?' I ask.

'Yes,' she blushes.

'Happy Birthday!' I say and she thanks me.

'It's actually tomorrow. But thank you. I think I should go now,' she says. 'Dad must be really bored.'

I nod, and then realize she can't see. So I say 'okay' and she steps down from the stool. Her dad's still watching.

'Can you walk me to my dad?'

'You think that's a great idea?' I ask, nervous at walking

towards a girl's dad who's 99 per cent hard muscles, 1 per cent eyes.

'Okay. I will go on my own then.'

I feel bad when I see her start to walk for she's petite as a bunny and the crowd is doing a stampede of stallions and I say, 'I will come.'

She reaches out to my outstretched arm and holds it and we walk towards her dad, who's still chatting with a bouncer, with one eye on us.

As soon as we get to him, he reaches out to her and hugs her, 'Did you have fun?'

'As much as I could!' she says and laughs.

'Who's your friend?' he asks and extends his hand. We shake hands.

'Deep,' I say before she, whose name I do not know yet, tells him that she doesn't know my name and he punches me into oblivion.

'He's staying in the same hotel as ours,' she adds.

'I'm her dad,' he says and then looks at her. 'But, Ahana, it's not yet twelve! On my eighteenth birthday I emptied bottles of Chivas Regal like it was water and danced till it was noon of the next day. Why don't you buy your friend a drink?'

'I don't drink, sir,' I say, silently adding, 'usually.' I hope he can't smell the alcohol on me; not the best first impression.

'What's wrong with kids these days?' he shakes his head.

'Fine, Dad, I will dance,' she says. 'But only if you don't look. Deep says your muscularity makes him nervous.'

The man laughs. It's a very masculine laugh, affected and practised, yet somehow very natural. I hate his perfectness.

'Fine. I will go hide myself some place.'

'Aren't you the best dad, leaving your daughter to dance with a stranger, oh, not before asking her to get drunk and dance till midnight?' she chuckles.

Her dad reaches for her hand and kisses it. 'I really have no choice. I have the best daughter in the world and that's a lot to live up to!'

He goes back to the bouncer and they walk away from us.

'Your dad is friends with the bouncer.'

'He makes friends easily. I don't.'

I beg to differ.

We are sitting on the pavement. The dancing, the music, the drunken theatrics, the excessive hugging is on like it just started; the party also looks like it has just started. There appears to be a carnival on the streets.

She tells me she's not much of dancer and I tell her I know exactly what that feels like.

She's doodling with her fingers on the pavement, her head still bobbing to the distant beats of dub step; she is smiling. For a girl who can't see herself in the mirror, she's dressed up nicely, a loose, long-sleeved pink shirt and shiny black pants; reminds me of the vampires with no reflections but impeccable hair and stuff.

'Deep, right?' she asks. 'What are you doing in Hong Kong? I'm sure my dad will ask.'

I tell her about my project of developing cataloguing software for libraries and then she asks me if I love books, and I say I can't imagine a world without them, and then she tells me she misses reading. She tells me it's been more than a year that she's been in Hong Kong, and I ask her if she loves it here, and she nods.

'It's a great place for a blind person,' she murmurs. 'How's it for someone who can see?'

'It is nothing like what I have seen before,' I answer honestly.

'It's not even funny how many questions Dad will ask me about you.'

'What will you say?'

'That you're not my type.'

I'm a little offended, even though it's a joke, but I say, 'You're not my type either. You're majorly exquisite.'

'Exquisite?' She laughs. 'You know a lot of strange words. Do you see him?'

'I'm sure he's on the top of some building aiming his sniper-type rifle at me.' I look around and he's not there. 'I can't see him.'

'Do you want to . . . maybe dance?' she asks, biting her nails.

'I think the people I came with left me alone because they saw me dancing,' I say, laughing.

She tell me it's okay, but I can see it in her blue-green eyes that she's sad and then I warn her that I'm a bad dancer and she says she wouldn't know because she's blind and she says it like she has acne or bad hair. She bets me that she's even worse, and I don't believe her.

I lead us towards the crowd that is dancing on the street, and I am shouting, 'Excuse me! Excuse me!' and I feel kind of important. We are bang in the middle of a scene from *Grease*. It's the centre of the street and everyone's dancing and everyone's cool and has great hair, none better than hers though!

We start shifting our weight awkwardly from one foot to another, I am consciously trying not to touch her, and she's looking straight, approximately at my abdominal area.

'Can you hold me? I feel like you're not there,' she asks like it's nothing, like I go about holding beautiful girls all the time. And just like that, my hands are on her waist. She's moving rather exquisitely like a snake to a charm, unhindered and graceful and just, just, incredibly hot! Her eyes are closed, her hands are playing with her hair, falling on her face, and I'm like half-dead and half in love, and her head sways like it's floating in the music, and she's some place else, somewhere far away. I want to tell her that she's a liar and a part-time belly dancer but I keep shut. I'm sure her dad's looking.

Seconds pass, then minutes, and she's still dancing, and I am still holding her, all my nerves seem to have accumulated in my palm for it feels so real, so immediate, like she's a cliff and I'm hanging on to her for life.

And just then the clock strikes twelve.

'Happy birthday, Ahana!'

'Thank you so much!' she says and adds shyly. 'You're an exquisite boy. Is the word gender-specific?'

'No!'

Her father soon comes and he's happier, also slightly drunk. He thanks me, and whisks her away. She walks with a cane that she sweeps around in front of her, people part like she's plagued.

I catch a cab and go back to my hotel, ride the lift alone and go to bed. She's in the next room, just a few walls away and the knowledge is unsettling.

# 13

I wake up to Ritik's call. He apologizes for having left me alone and then metaphorically nudges me, saying I had game yesterday, and that the girl I 'picked' was pretty. He asks me who the 'old guy' was, and I ignore the question. I ask him if I have to come to office again, and he says no one cares, and then laughs and disconnects the call. I promptly go back to sleep as if I never picked up the call and soon I'm dreaming the same dream I was before the phone rang.

It's ten when I wake up, find that my toothbrush has been replaced by a brand new one, so I brush enthusiastically, and then more vigorously because I might bump into the girl from yesterday. It strikes me then that she's blind, but I still brush harder, just in case.

I have just one shirt left. Blind. Blind. Blind. I tell myself. It puts me at ease knowing that she doesn't know I'm a gangly idiot who stares awkwardly at her. She just knows I smell old, so I shower like a POW coming back home after a decade.

In the shower, where all great ideas emerge, I'm thinking of H.G. Wells's *The Country of the Blind* where everyone's blind and the concepts of beauty and ugliness are obsolete. But people do smell. I empty another bottle of bathing gel.

Then I find out that the breakfast is complimentary. I didn't know that before. I have wasted two days' worth of food and this knowledge would make my mom angry.

It's a buffet and it smells nothing like Mom's cooking, but it still smells great; like the sea has descended into the restaurant. The smell is raw and fresh, yet the open flames are blazing. I want to eat everything to make up for the two days that I missed, the stir fried noodles, the ramen bowls, the pasta, EVERYTHING!

It doesn't take me long to spot her, sitting in the corner seat, slurping noodles into her mouth from the bowl. She's good with chopsticks. She's still in her pyjamas, and they are white and pink, her golden brown hair is all over her face, and it's unfairly adorable.

I fill up a bowl with shrimps, ramen and chicken, and it smells delicious.

'Can I join you?'

'Huh?' She pulls out the earphones from her ears. 'Oh! It's you. You smell of seafood today!'

'I bathed extra-hard today.'

She is giggling and then she asks, 'Are you sitting?'

'Yes, I am.'

'I expected to meet you today,' she says. A piece of chicken slips from the chopsticks and falls into the bowl, and splatters. 'I always have breakfast in my room. Today Dad insisted we eat here. He must have known that you eat here.'

'But why?'

'Because he's now my enthusiastic girlfriend trying to set me up with you.'

'Your dad is a mixed martial arts fighter, a cold-blooded killer, not a girlfriend.'

'I'm sure he's around, keeping an eye on me. But I think he likes you. Last night, he kept talking about you as if you're his newest crush,' she says. Then she suddenly changes the topic, 'Chopsticks suck! So blind-person-insensitive. I'm done!' She slides her bowl away from her; in silent protest against blind-insensitive chopsticks. I drop my chopsticks too and use the fork instead. I see her Dad sitting a few tables away, talking animatedly to two men—all of them are dressed in dark suits and shiny shoes.

'I can see your dad. He's sitting with two other men. Looks like a Secret Service meeting to me.'

'You can stop worrying about him! He's not bad. And I told you he likes you.'

'But can he kill a boy sitting twenty feet away?' I ask, only half-joking.

'I'm sure he has done that from longer distances.'

'With chopsticks?'

'I doubt he's that good.'

I eat quickly, trying to forget my kung-fu mastery over chopsticks from yesterday, and I almost choke on my food.

'Are you okay?'

'I think a shrimp just jumped back to life in my throat. I'm done too.'

I push my bowl to the centre of the table as well and our bowls touch, and it makes me uneasy, the butterflies-in–the-stomach uneasy, the roller-coaster-that-has–no-bottom uneasy, the best type of uneasy.

'Oh shit! Your dad is coming over,' I utter in panic as I puff up my chest. I don't know why but probably to look like I'm not all bones.

'Are you kids having fun?' he asks and looks mostly at her. He scoops her up in his large hands, and she looks like a stuffed toy, the kind that's too precious to be sent into mass production.

'He was wondering if you could kill men with chopsticks.'

'I have killed with less,' he laughs and then adds, 'I just test pilot small planes and sometimes cargo planes. It's boring. Its been years since I have had the imponderable joy of seeing a man die.' I'm not sure if he's joking but they laugh so I guess it's a joke. He says, 'I have a meeting to go to, Ahana. Are you sure you will be okay? Deep, do you have somewhere to be today?' he asks, his movie-star eyes are compelling and I say, 'No!'

'Oh, Dad. Stop it! I will be fine.'

'What? I was just saying that you need to treat him on your birthday. That's all!' he defends himself. 'Fine, Deep. If you have anything else to do, you can. She can celebrate her birthday on her own.'

'No, sir, I am doing nothing today.'

'See?' her dad says and Ahana rolls her eyes.

He leaves with his friends from the Secret Service and I breathe easy.

'Why do you call him sir?' Ahana asks and gets up from the table. She knocks over a bottle of Tabasco sauce.

'I think I want him to like me.'

We walk to her room, her fingers are wrapped around my arm and I don't think I will ever get used to her touch. We ride the elevator together. She's standing next to me, my arm in her hands.

She is mumbling and I realize she's counting the steps to her room. She unlocks her room and I let her hand go and stand at the entrance. She enters.

'You can come in. I will not tell Dad,' she giggles.

'What makes you think I will take that chance? I'm sure he has the whole place bugged and is sitting in a black van running facial recognition and background checks on me.'

'God! You do have a superhuman imagination. And it's okay. I asked him. You're allowed in our room.'

'Are you sure?'

'Positive.'

'You're answerable to my parents if something happens to me. There are no spare parts to replace me in my family.'

'You're impossible!' And she adds, 'In a good way.'

'What happened here?' I ask. Vases lie broken on the floor, there are pillows torn open, and lamps lie upturned on the floor.

'My mood swing last evening.'

'It swung like a cyclone.'

'Don't make fun of me. I'm a poor blind girl and no one's allowed to be mean to me. It's one of the perks of being blind.'

'Um—'

'It still sucks.'

Gingerly, she walks to her bed and sits down, and then lies down and sighs. Her room is huge. It's actually a corner suite with two rooms and two bathrooms and countless lights and two televisions. There's even a black shiny piano in the corner.

'Do you play the piano?' I ask.

'Yes, but I kind of suck.'

'Play!' I urge.

She refuses but I insist and walk her to the piano. She asks me to sit next to her on the piano stool and I do so. I can feel her close to me and I find it difficult to breathe.

'Be kind to me.' She starts playing what she tells me is Rachmaninoff's Second Piano Sonata, 1913 edition, which I know is one of the toughest pieces to play (I read it in the memoir of a pianist who killed himself) and she's surprised that I know.

I'm not an expert on music, but her fingers dexterously move on the keys and it sounds perfect.

'You're such a liar!' I say to her. She's smiling like she knows she's nailed it. 'You said you can't dance and you dance like you majored in it, and you play the piano like it's your pet. I will never believe you now,' I act as if I'm angry.

'I'm sorry, I've never thought I'm good enough! Okay, what can I play for you?'

'Play something I recognize,' I say.

She plays a medley of old Hindi songs, and I recognize the tunes from the tapes of my dad, who is a great fan of old Hindi instrumentals. It's been years since Mom has been trying to get him to clear out the drawers filled with hundreds of cassettes, but Dad never listens to her and it's one of those rare occasions when they fight.

'That was great!' I exclaim.

She gets up, our bodies no longer touching, and I breathe easy. 'You're just saying that . . .'

'I'm not. It was concert-level great. You're a child prodigy, damn it!'

'It's easier for blind people to be prodigies. We are like little circus puppies. The littlest thing we do people go like, *hey, did you look at that, it can stand and sit.* It isn't flattering at all!'

'I didn't—'

She sighs and buries her face in her palms. 'I'm so sorry. It's just that being blind is like constantly PMSing.'

'That's a great quote!'

She laughs and the tension evaporates. We are silent. She keeps thinking of something and smiles, throwing her hair back, which is about six million shades of brown right now.

'Deep. I'm sorry for Dad, but if you have to be somewhere you can go. It's fine by me.'

'There is nowhere I would rather be than right here.'

She smiles. I'm the freaking tsunami!

14

I have never believed that I will ever write a novel, or get published, or win the Michael J. Printz award for Best Young Adult Fiction, or date a supermodel, or run for Prime Minister some day, but I also didn't think I would be in the hotel suite of a girl who makes you think of promises and forevers and cute puppies and double rainbows.

Neither did I know I would be picking out clothes for her.

'Dad buys all my clothes for me. He shuffles through fashion magazines and tells me the colour. Please don't tell me he makes me look like a great, big joke.'

'Oh, shut up! This closet looks like a socialite's wardrobe! If I sell it off I will have enough to put in a bank in Switzerland. I can't even figure out what goes where. Wait! I think I found a T-shirt!'

I hand over the T-shirt to her and she holds it near her nose. 'I got it in Paris. I can smell it.'

'And then you say you're not a circus puppy! No offence.'

'None taken.'

I choose a pair of pants; she says it's too long and we settle on something shorter. She takes a shower and changes.

'Are you sure you want to go out?' she asks.

'Yes, I'm sure. You need to give me a treat! Moreover, I'm not comfortable staying here. It feels like your dad's watching.'

'I find it hard to keep up when people walk fast,' she says quietly.

'I'm in no hurry.'

We leave the hotel and find ourselves on the busy street. She takes her cane out and starts tapping it in front of her. She holds me with her other hand. People part in front of us, staying clear of her cane—they all look. Oh. My. God. They are all looking. People are looking at her, and me, their face contorting in pity, or maybe in relief that they are not like her. I'm furious, my fists are clenched, and I want to shout at them that they are nothing like her! And that she is my favourite person in the world!

I calm down when I see people helping us out, and smiling, and giving us the right of way in lifts and escalators and pathways.

'Are you embarrassed?' she asks. I look at her angrily, but then I melt because a) she's ignorant of what she has come to mean to me and b) she's a dewdrop, beautiful and fresh and impossible to describe!

'You're the most extraordinary thing to have happened to me overseas!'

'Overseas, huh?' she mocks me. We find ourselves a seat on the Metro and she folds her cane and keeps it in her handbag. 'You must be some kind of playboy, Deep. You're likeable, you don't drink, you read books and you're brilliant enough to be sent for a trip to Hong Kong, all paid for, no less.'

'I'm no dating expert, but girls want none of that.'

'Girls are blind.'

It takes me a few seconds to get the pun. And to figure out where we are going.

'Where are we going?' I ask.

'Hollywood Street. Man Mo temple.'

'Temple? Why a temple?'

I unfold a map of Hong Kong that I always carry in my pocket and start looking for the street we are on. The names of streets are straight out of a Hollywood movie, sprinkled with liberal dosages of age-old oriental kung-fu. Cleverly Street, Queen's Road Central and Staunton Street criss-cross on the same map with Wing Lok Street and Lok Ku Road, quite like Hong Kong itself, which is a cauldron brimming with people of innumerable nationalities, all of whom bring with them their cultures, which is then readily adopted and moulded and shared, till it fossilizes with the rest of Hong Kong, making it the perfect melange of colours and cultures. No wonder you would find an Indonesian and a French restaurant jostling for space between an authentic Chinese medicinal tea outlet and a street food stall selling the famed Hong Kong waffle and lobster balls and preserved eggs. As I'm thinking all of this, I get hungry, and Ahana and I share a chunk of freshly barbequed pork with rice we buy off a street stall.

Soon we are down and on the street. Our task—to visit a two-hundred–year-old temple hidden in the recesses of the all-pervasive high-rises.

'Get us a taxi,' she says and I wave to stop one. She tells the driver to take us to the Man Mo temple. The driver nods and says, 'Okay, okay, I take you, okay, okay!' enthusiastic and chirpy. He bows twice, which I assume is a gesture to say he's thankful and that's strange because I should be thankful that he's taking us there. I can get used to this. People in Hong Kong—from the taxi drivers to the shopkeepers to the waiters at restaurants are constantly smiling and thanking you, and it's slowly spoiling me.

'I thought I will take you some place which will help you write your book.'

I search but I can't recall if I have ever told her about the book. 'When did I tell you about the book?' I ask.

'I guessed. You read so many of them, so I thought you would want, some time in life, to write one yourself.'

'How will the temple help me write? I don't think I'm the visit-strange-places-for-inspiration kind of writer. I'm mostly a stare-at-a-blank-computer-screen-and-then-curse type of writer. On second thoughts, I'm mostly a writer who doesn't write.'

'I'm starting to love the idea of you being a writer.'

'Welcome to the club!'

'I like writers.'

'Here,' the driver says and we step down.

The little red and golden temple with sloping green roofs on which small dragons are perched or hanging precariously, is nestled on a street surrounded by much newer buildings. Its entrance is guarded by statues of what looks like a pride of lions; the lions can also be seen in different areas around the magnificent temple, She tells me that 'Man' is the God of Literature and 'Mo' is the God of War.

'It's beautiful,' I tell her.

'Ideally, you should have been here with my dad. Both your gods are here.'

'There is just one God.'

'But isn't it great that he's like ice cream? You can pick a flavour you like and it will still be ice and cream,' she says. 'No one can tell you which flavour to like.'

As I climb up the little stairs to the temple, suddenly the unrelenting traffic and noise of the city die out. Inside the complex it is like time stops here; it's calm and it's quiet, except for a murmur of prayers that floats around us, carrying us further away from the urgent bustle of the city.

She follows close behind, holding my hand, yet gauging the steps.

'Tell me what you see? It smells paradisiacal.'

'Even I don't know what that word means,' I say.

'Tell me.'

I look around the temple and find that, except for the people around us, everything is old, really, really old. 'The walls are painted red and engraved with red and golden coloured inscriptions and paintings. It's beautiful! There is incense all around, which I'm sure you can smell. There are giant incense coils that are hanging from the ceiling, burning away slowly. So many! Look!' I exclaim and then shut up.

'How many are there?'

'Like only about three million. They are hanging everywhere! There are also golden urns in which incense sticks are stuck, some as thick as my arm. Do you want to light some?'

'I want the ones as thick as your arm,' she beams.

We buy a few incense sticks, the ones as thick as my arm, and light them in an open fire. A woman tells her that every stick has to be lighted before it can be offered to the gods.

'How do the gods look?'

'Like gods,' I say. 'Staring down at us. They kind of look angry. I get why the God of War is angry, it's probably in his job description, but why's the God of Literature angry?'

'Because they're still ice and cream.'

We leave our incense sticks in one of the urns. 'Take me where I can pray,' she says and I hold her hand and make her sit down where a few women were talking to themselves. Periodically, they throw two semi-circular wooden pieces in front of them. I tell Ahana what they are doing and Ahana asks one of the women. The woman explains, 'You ask him a question. The wooden pieces are dice and they tell you if your wish would come true or not.'

'That sounds like fun,' she says, closes her eyes, mumbles something and throws the pieces in front of her. It's a no. I hand her back the pieces. She tries again, mumbles a longer sentence, and it's a no again. The third time it's a yes.

I try it too and it turns out to be a no; I stop trying.

We leave the temple after walking around a bit, soaking in the 'paradisiacal' atmosphere, as she put it.

'What did you ask for?' I ask her.

'Wishes are not supposed to be told. They don't come true otherwise,' she snaps.

'Tell me the ones which aren't coming true.'

'I'm not going to see in the nearest future. And Dad's not to stop trying to get me to see again,' she says. She looks in my direction with her saddened eyes. I want to hug her but I don't know if it's appropriate.

'I don't see a point in asking God for stuff! It's a business strategy. You ask for something, the pieces say no, you buy more incense sticks and beg him to turn it into a yes, and the cycle goes on. I don't think he cares. God is maybe a really high-maintenance, attention-seeking woman,' I say, and add, 'but at least you got the last one right.'

'The last one was for you,' she says. 'But I can't tell you what it was.'

'For me?'

'God doesn't want us to beg. Maybe God wants us to wish for good things for other people, and maybe that's the point of worship. Maybe God *is* a woman, but an old mother looking for a little bit of love,' she says and adds after a second, 'What did you ask for?'

I don't answer.

15

Walking on the Hollywood Road (the closest I would ever get to Hollywood, although life does have a strange way of surprising me these days), I'm wondering how easily I have warmed up to the idea to walking with a girl holding my hand. I have held hands with a girl before, but it feels different. I'm as scared to let it go as I'm joyous about holding it in the present.

'There's a graffiti on the wall which I think is of a dog or a sheep and it's wearing a mask that's connected to a plant that's strapped to its back,' I explain. I really like explaining things to her. It feels like the only thing I have ever done that matters.

'That has to be one thoughtful bad-ass teenager graffiti artist,' she says.

'Bad-ass teenager graffiti artist.'

'What?'

'It sounds so cool!'

We walk lazily up and down the streets, occasionally walking into a quaint shop that seemed to have jumped out of picture postcards from Venice or Amsterdam. I find it hard to tell her what they sell because these shops are like little museums selling history; antique pieces lie around to be bought and they are beautiful and they can be touched, and when she touches them and says, 'I just shook hands with someone from hundred years ago!' her face glows, and her eyes brighten.

I see things yet I can't experience them like she does. I don't think of them as 'Bad-ass teenager graffiti art' or that I've 'shaken hands with a person from hundreds of years ago'.

We idle along the Hollywood Road and I describe to her the buildings whose grandiose designs are interestingly colonial, one of which—as I later learn is the old Hong Kong police headquarters—is marked as a heritage site on my map. She tells me it's because we are on the second oldest road in Hong Kong laid by Royal Marine Engineers over a hundred and fifty years ago.

Later, we walk to a restaurant that serves Korean food, and she tells me she loves Korean food and how it smells. I read out from the menu and she orders for both of us.

'I must warn you that what you just ordered doesn't look so nice,' I tell her, looking suspiciously at the pictures on the menu card.

'If you were to just feel your food without being able to see it, you wouldn't eat half the things you like,' she says like a saint.

'I have a crush on your blind wisdom!' I laugh.

The food arrives and I have to give it to her that it tastes pretty good. I'm used to food where spices are all you taste, but here I can actually taste every ingredient individually.

We walk out of the restaurant and I thank her for paying and she tries to slap me but misses.

'Call a taxi?' I ask. She nods, and when I ask if we are going back to the hotel, she shakes her head and tells me that she needs me to do something for her. The word *need* never felt so powerful before.

'Is it okay if I call a friend?' she asks.

'Is it a girl? Because I'm wearing a shirt that's over three hundred years old and never once washed. It's the reason why I smell old.'

'It's a guy. And he's blind as well. We are like the three musketeers only that we are just two and we don't have swords or eyes or people to fight.'

'Ahana, you're funny. And not girl funny. Like guy funny, like stand-up comic funny.'

'And you just know the right things to say to a blind girl,' she flutters her eyelashes.

'I have been known to be a charmer,' I respond. 'So much so that it's like girls have a restraining order to keep away from me lest they find themselves falling hopelessly in love with me. My good looks are only known to blind people.'

'Only blind people are allowed blind jokes,' she answers. 'It's in the constitution of blind people which no one else but we can read because it's in Braille,' she laughs.

Our taxi takes us to the Central Garden Station, from where the Peak Tram starts, a train that goes up into the mountains. Ahana tells me that there is an unbelievable view to be admired on the way. Of all the trams that criss–cross across the landscape of Hong Kong, giving it an old–world charm, this is the only one that climbs uphill.

She calls her friend and he says he will be there, no questions asked.

'It's like a really slow rollercoaster that wouldn't come

down, but stops at the top,' she says. 'I have heard people say, 'Look at that,' and then there are many sounds of cameras clicking. I can hear people smile.'

'I will let you know what all the noise is about.' She nods happily. I'm excited too.

The tram starts on a plane, and then suddenly and almost perilously, it's inclined at an awkward angle that trains shouldn't be inclined at, let alone be trudging slowly at.

'This is a little scary,' I say.

'That would be a first. I have never heard someone say that in the tram.'

'We will continue the conversation as if I hadn't said anything about the scariness,' I say. 'Man! This is good though. We have left trees behind, which now look tilted, also I see buildings that are tilted—everything's kind of inclined! This is so weird. Oh! I also see the sea! It's like Newton's frame of reference. How we see things depend on where we are.'

'It took Newton to say that? They could have just asked me!'

'Oh, your sexy blind jokes,' I say. It's the first time I have used the word 'sexy' with a girl.

'Aren't you just the stud?'

'I'm every girl's dream!' I say expansively. Soon we've reached the top.

Holding hands, we walk out and it's 'Hong Kong on the mountain' all over again. There is a McDonald's outlet, sushi restaurants, and people selling nail paints and giving free hairstyles. Ahana opts for a hair makeover and once she is done she asks me if it looks any good and I just nod vigorously and she somehow hears the eager nod. We walk to the Sky

Terrace, which is famous for a birds'-eye view of the island. Our tickets are torn and we take the escalator. My fear of heights is slowly kicking in.

'What it is like?' she asks.

'It's like flying. It's really up there. Everything is tiny, like really tiny. It's not a birds'-eye view. I don't think even they fly this high in the air.'

'Do you like it?'

'I'm still a little scared. I think I suffer from every kind of phobia there is,' I say and she reaches for my hand. We walk around the edge slowly, and I feel okay. Everything feels okay with her.

'It's alright. I will not let go,' she clutches my hand tighter. She reminds me of my mom and of when I was eight and we were on the giant wheel, I was scared out of my wits, and Dad, who was Superman to me, laughed, and I wanted to emulate him and Mom whispered in my ears, 'You're stronger,' and that made everything alright.

We are walking around, slowly and cautiously, as if the wind would consume me and throw me past the ledge if I am not careful, when her phone rings and I spot a guy—he is unbelievably hot! I don't want to be mean or insensitive, but Ahana and he are like model children from a property advertisement—too pretty to be less than anything but perfect.

He is walking without a stick, though I'm sure there is one in his bag. He's making clicking sounds that I can hear from afar.

'He's pretty buff for a blind kid,' I say, amazed.

'I wouldn't know,' she says. Then he is near us and she says, 'Hi!'

'You reflect sound like a koala bear! Have you gained

weight? Happy Birthday!' he rattles off and hugs her. It's an awkward hug, hands and arms going everywhere, but once they find the groove, it lasts long enough to make me feel uncomfortable.

'You must be Deep. I'm Aveek,' he says, his hand hangs in the air and I shake it.

'He was just telling me what it feels like to be here. He says it's like flying,' she tells him.

'Let's sit,' Aveek says, and grabs her arm and starts making the clicking sound again. They sit on a bench and I follow. 'My father tells me it feels like a bird shitting on a skyscraper,' he says.

'Well, Deep is a writer,' she says, 'and you're just an eternal pessimist.'

'I'm not really a writer,' I correct.

'How have you been?' he asks Ahana, and they are still holding hands. 'Is your Dad still being a jerk?'

'He's not a jerk. He's just concerned and hopeful.'

'He's just stupid!' Aveek says. 'If I were you I would ask him to shut up and let you be the way you are. Why the fuck fight it? He needs to accept you.'

'Shut up. He loves me!' Ahana defends her dad. They are still holding hands. This isn't good.

'No, he doesn't! He just drags you around wherever he thinks he can get you to see and I don't see that happening,' he says.

'I can't ask him to lose all hope, Aveek!'

'You're just weak,' Aveek says arrogantly, like he's a mutant urging her to accept her situation. 'Do you want to eat something? I'm starving!'

I do not exist any more. She says yes. They walk. I follow

them to Bubba Gump, which looks distinctly like the TGIF I once went to when my father was promoted to Head Librarian; Mom had complained about the food and how much it cost and how she could have cooked much better food at home. I had concurred.

Aveek and Ahana sit on one side of the table, still holding hands, and I sit on the other, clenching my fists in discomfort. Aveek excuses himself because he says he needs to make space for beer.

I want to ask her, 'Who the hell is this arrogant asshole?' but instead I ask, 'Who's he?' We aren't close enough to act possessive.

'I used to date him,' she says. 'Aveek visits Hong Kong frequently because of his seminars, and I have been living here for the last eighteen months, so our paths crossed. My father really liked him. Well, he likes every guy who kind of talks to me. But Dad thought we were a nice fit. He's blind since birth but he's kind of a genius. He makes these clicking sounds,' she says and clicks with her mouth, her lips pucker and it's irresistible, 'and it echoes back to him and he knows where he's going. It's called echo navigation. He's one of the few blind people who know how to use it. It's pretty awesome!'

But I'm still stuck on her first sentence. 'You used to date him?'

'Yes. Dad used to get along with him. They used to work out together,' she says. 'But we broke up because of his negative thoughts. So Dad wanted me to stay away from him, said he was a bad influence, a dampener. I didn't agree at first, but broke up with him later, not because he was a bad influence, but because he was always too good, and too busy for me. His eyes were cut out when he was just a few months old. Retinal cancer. And he's used to his blindness, and he wants me to get used to my blindness too.'

'I like your Dad.'

Aveek comes back and takes over the conversation. 'I think we should order two platters. I really need to bulk up these days because I think my strength is going down.'

'You seem pretty strong,' I say, trying to participate in the conversation because I am treated worse than the waiter.

'Oh, I'm so weak. Almost like her father!' he jokes. Neither of us finds it funny. Aveek continues, 'He wears medium size, imagine that. Do you ever work out, Deep?'

'He writes,' Ahana interrupts.

'Lame,' he says. The food arrives and he knows exactly where the waitress is standing; he thanks her and shoots a smile at her. He reminds me of Aman if Aman were to behave like a prick. He's blind and everything, and a cancer survivor, but I still hate him. I feel guilty about it, but I still hate him.

The conversation shifts to blind people stuff. They talk about the blind conventions they used to go to, the new Facebook-friendly Braille tablet, of how the new lift systems are much more accessible, and how the street light sounds aren't loud enough. Then he tells her about his trip to the US where he taught people his extraordinary ability to echo navigate. 'The girls were falling all over me! My sound waves were echoing the word, slut, slut, slut, slut,' he says.

I eat in silence.

The bill comes on the table and he almost snatches it from me. 'Let me pay. You're still a student.'

I insist reluctantly and we split the bill two ways; he still insists that he pays for Ahana. Ahana stays quiet.

We take the Peak Tram back to the main city and exit the Metro station. I'm still waiting for Aveek to tell us that he needs to go somewhere.

'Hey, I know this really cool place with new gadgets for us!' he says excitedly. 'They are showcasing some concept cars and stuff like that. We should totally go.'

'Okay,' Ahana says. 'I still have time I think. Do you want to come with us, Deep?'

'What will he do there? Let him carry on!' he says and thrusts his hand out, and before I can say anything, he adds, 'Good to meet you, Deep.'

He grabs her hand and they walk away.

Part Two

The Blind Girl

16

I can't see.

I know Dad's tall, but when I was small, everyone was tall and towered above me. I also remember him as being strong-jawed and muscular, but it can also be because that's all I hear about him. Mom's like a painting, and that's not even a simile, she's literally like a painting seared in my memory. I identify colours from her image in my head. Blue is the colour of her eyes, brown her hair, light brown is the colour of her skin, and white is the colour of the knee-length dress she wears.

I now wish I had paid more attention during the first five years of my life to seeing everything around me rather than trying to learn to walk or be potty trained. But then I had no idea I was going to go blind and would have to search in the nooks of my memory whenever someone mentioned a colour or a shape or estimation of size. Or at least my blindness should have come with a notice period. It's frustrating to learn that I could have known what the seven wonders of the world looked like, if only someone had cared to show me those in pictures! This wouldn't have happened if I had some notice.

But I do know that Mom was beautiful and I miss her.

Life's hard without her, but Dad is always around and that's a mixed bag. He used to be like this free-spirited eagle and now he's like a kitten, always scared, because he has to tend to a blind girl, yours truly, and make sure she's not getting run over by buses etc. I really spoil his game.

You would think I remember everything I saw before the age of five, since I have never seen anything after that, but you can't be farther from the truth. Slowly, every image sort of faded away and transformed into sounds and smells; I rarely even see dreams these days, they are mostly just sounds.

Aveek's tugging at my hand. He always walks too fast for my comfort and never lets me use my cane whenever I'm with him. He's a little too confident for his own good, but I stopped saying that when my dog, Bruno, got run over by a truck and Aveek just told me, 'He was always a disaster. I never liked guide dogs.' I had just hung up the phone and cried the night alone. Well, not alone. Dad kept ordering chicken soup for me, which did taste rather brilliant. Dad's like Oprah—he handles crying girls with amazing tenacity. And that's because he, unfortunately, had a lot of training, raising me.

I hate trucks. They are monstrous. But Dad tells me to imagine trucks to be just as big as cars, even though for me cars are pretty big too, because I was hardly a few centimetres tall when I last saw one.

'Who's your friend?' Aveek asks, clicking and trying to

locate the edge of the pavement. He succeeds and then even manages to stop a taxi: little feats that make him the Edward Cullen of my life, unbelievable and extraordinary. 'Buff for a blind kid', as Deep put it.

Aveek is a star in the kingdom of the blind. He's the golden boy, the Lance Armstrong (from pre-doping scandal days) of our world, the cancer survivor who sees with his ears.

Every blind school he goes to, every convention he attends, he's the star attraction. Not only is he fiercely independent for a blind person, I have heard he's gorgeous, built like a tree, and talks like a talk-show host. His motivational speeches are a big hit, and not only with blind people. Blind girls find their panties in a bunch when they hear his name. His conventions are always sold off, the majority of the crowd being teenage, legally blind girls.

I met him in the US, where Dad took me, because he heard from a friend of a friend that a research institute had a breakthrough regarding LCA, and that gene therapy could help blind people like me. Dad never misses the slightest chance to whisk me away to places with possibilities. (And with cargo and light planes to test.)

I really don't mind, because I'm used to living in hotels ever since Mom died and I get accustomed to bumping into new things pretty often. Also, different accents excite me.

Aveek was giving a lecture, which was an hour-long rant about his struggle with cancer and blindness, and God, was he charming! I had heard about him before from the other blind girls in Malaysia, where Dad worked for a year, while I studied. They thought I would know him since he was a fellow Indian.

At the high tea after the conference, which was in a huge

hall full of the barks of guide dogs and tapping sounds of canes, Dad had walked up to Aveek, with me in tow. I had felt my cheeks go warm.

'This is my daughter,' Dad had said and made us shake hands. 'She uses a guide dog.'

'After sufficient training in echo navigation, she will not have to use a dog,' he had said in a voice that sounded even better than it did on the microphone. He sounded like undaunted hopes and dreams and courage and I was hopelessly in love with him. It was like a fan meeting her hero. What do you expect?

I don't know what he heard in me, but we ended up spending the evening together. He tried to teach me his clicks, but he was the Zen master and I was a stupid student lost in his voice, in his audacity, and I soaked in his reflected glory.

When he kissed me that night, it felt wet and unhygienic, but maybe that's how blind-people kisses feel (or maybe even non-blind ones, but I have no way of finding out), and that's how the two other kisses with legally blind boys felt, but at least his lips were soft and chewing-gummy. There was none of the passion or the heat or the heavy sighs that I had heard of in audio books, but there was a sense of achievement. He liked me and that was enough.

We reach the convention centre and he makes me sit on a couch that is a little too soft for my comfort and I sink in.

'I will be back in bit. I have to meet some people,' he says.

Then, he kisses me on my cheek. He still does that and I think he shouldn't, but he's usually done by the time I realize it's happening, so I never see the point of protesting.

Half an hour passes by and he's not back yet. For an eighteen-year-old blind boy, he sure has a lot of people to meet. But then again I forget, he's the golden boy, and I'm just a regular girl with a handicap.

I'm fiddling with my phone, listening to all the tweets from celebrities around the world. It's become my number one way to kill time ever since someone made an application which brings Twitter to blind people. And also, you get to know so much about nipple slips and explicit pictures leaked on the Internet. It's entertaining because I literally can't understand the noise about it. If my naked pictures go online, I would probably go like, 'Do I at least look good?'

'Are you okay?' he nudges me. Before I can respond he says, 'I'm sorry, I'm really stuck. I have to meet someone.' He leaves me again.

When he comes back, he finds me sleeping on the couch, and wakes me up. I'm listening to the audio book of *Huckleberry Finn*, which is playing in a loop for the third time.

'You were listening to a book? Did your writer friend put to up to this?' he asks as I sense him putting one of the ends of the earphone to his ear. 'It's sped up! What's it like? Like 900 words per minute?'

'It's 1000 words per minute,' I correct him.

'Lame.'

It's the only thing I do better than Aveek; words come at slow motion to me. (Like most blind people, we have higher than usual comprehension of the spoken word.)

What you hear on the radio as, 'Investment in mutual funds

involves risk and the offer documents of the funds should be read for further details,' we hear as, 'Investment . . . in . . . mutual . . . funds . . . involves . . . risk . . . and . . . the . . . offer . . . documents . . . of . . . the . . . funds . . . should . . . be . . . read . . . for . . . further . . . details.'

I think I have a career in deciphering rap lyrics.

We are in the taxi again. I get to see none of the exhibits that he promised we would. He probably tried a lot of them and I will probably listen to his quotes on some new blind product after a couple of months.

I really loved him. I think I still do. How could I not? It would be like a high school graduate complaining that Justin Bieber doesn't spend enough time with her! Ours was a long-distance relationship and though he kept coming over to Hong Kong in the past year, it was never enough for me. But it was always enough for him.

My girlfriends from my old school told me I was crazy for breaking up with someone who flew down from wherever he used to tour just to be with me, but I knew I couldn't handle his absence or the insecurity of being with someone who was 'out of sight' and always amongst people who loved him dearly. I thought I wasn't good enough for him and he never made me feel otherwise. Then one day I told him Dad wanted me to stay away from him.

I had lost a dog and it had pained me terribly; I wasn't prepared for the pain of losing a boyfriend.

He dropped me home, and he held my hand the entire

way, which made me cry a little and wish we were still together. It made me hope he would tell me that he still needed me despite all that he had, that he really missed me and wanted me back, but he didn't.

# 17

I'm trying not to cry in the lift.

I have twenty-eight steps to wipe my face off anything that may suggest I have been crying. Also, I hope that Dad isn't in the room. I don't smell Deep around. The word 'old' came out very inappropriately the first time I sensed him; I wanted to say 'home' but I couldn't bring myself to say it. He smelled faintly like Mom, earthy and worn out and pleasant, quite unlike Aveek, who smells of new cars and expensive perfumes and hair gel and hotel lobbies.

My steps are slow and I'm sniffing like a narcotics dog trying to sense if Deep is around. I'm not crying, but I'm sad that Aveek is always there when I want him, and yet isn't there. And Deep . . . well I don't even know who is he. I unlock the door and I just know Dad is there, just like Bruno used to know when I was around even when I was minutes away.

'How has the birthday been?' he asks and walks up to me. I lose myself in his arms, which wrap around me twice.

'It was great!'

'Was it? Who were you with?' he asks, helping me sit

down on my bed. 'Deep has been in his room since the last couple of hours. Where were you? Don't tell me you were with Aveek again.'

'Chill, Dad! We were just hanging out,' I say, a bit coldly.

'I'm just saying the boy isn't to be trusted. He's often up to no good. You have been hurt once!' he cautions.

'I will be fine, trust me.'

'He's not a nice boy.'

'You mean to say he can find someone better, right? Thank you for the confidence you show in me.'

'I never said that,' he says quietly. He knows it's true.

'But that's exactly what you meant.'

I plug in my earphones and pretend that I'm listening to music. I would rather be invisible than be a problem child.

'Why did you leave Deep behind?' he asks. 'I know you're not listening to anything. I like him.'

I have had a long day, walking around, being confused why one boy is with me and why the other is not, and so I snap, 'But HE CAN SEE, DAD! Get over him and leave me alone.'

'I just thought you needed a friend,' he says apologetically.

'I DON'T NEED ANYONE! Stop feeling sorry for me,' I say and bury my face in a pillow and mumble into it. I'm cursing, and then I'm crying. Sometimes I just hate everyone around me, people who can see, people who can't, people who pity, people who try to be normal . . . everyone. They say they know me because they have met other blind people, as if being blind is the only way one can describe me, like it's my identity and it's all that needs to be taken care of. They don't understand that though walking around, bumping into people and trash cans might be a part of my life, it isn't all there is to it. I have other concerns as well.

Some days, I just want it to end. I don't want to die or anything, but I want it to stop. Dad's hopes, people treating me differently, the conventions for the visually impaired, other people like me talking about pain and courage—I just want it to stop and be a five-year-old all over again.

And then Dad's patting my head like only he can and I feel a lot calmer, my heart rate goes down but I don't want to stop yet. It feels so nice that I drift away to sleep. When I wake up, he's still sitting there, his hand on my head. I hate it because he makes things alright so easily; I hate it because he doesn't let me be as angry as I should be, I hate it that he's the perfect father and I'm the imperfect daughter.

'I'm sorry,' I mumble and turn to him. He kisses my forehead.

'You don't have to be sorry for anything. I went too far. You're a big girl,' he kisses me again, 'and you have the right to meet anyone you want.'

'I'm sorry you have to put up with me. You should have given me up to an orphanage. I would be much better off making candles.'

He hugs me tightly. 'NO! Don't say that. *Never* say that. I can't imagine my life without you. I can't even begin to think how . . . just . . . don't say that ever again,' he breathes. Dad never cries, but I always know when his machismo is in a civil war with his tear glands.

I nod my head silently, not trusting myself to speak. Thank God at least he can see.

'Let's go out for dinner?' he asks.

I smile, and all my fears dissipate in a moment. 'I wouldn't say no to the handsomest man I have ever seen now, would I?'

It's been over a year since Dad shifted to Hong Kong to test pilot some small and some cargo planes for companies, and I am yet to join a college or decide on a subject I want to study. Thinking, I step on the longest escalator ever made, like, ever.

'Isn't SoHo for older people?' I ask Dad because he always has his out-of-office meetings in the district.

'Are you asking that because I hang out there?' he asks, and I'm sure he's raising an eyebrow, but I have no way to tell.

'You know, kind of?'

'Are you saying I'm old? Ahana, I can pass off as your boyfriend any given day.'

'You can say anything to a midnight girl and she would believe it,' I say and he hugs me close.

He loves it when I call myself a midnight girl.

Dad used to be a big fan of comic books, and he named me Daredevil after the blind superhero, but the nickname was too masculine, so I chose *Midnight Girl*. Dr Midnight was another blind superhero, he wasn't famous or anything, but he was blind and that often came in the way of major superheroing. The comic series wasn't popular so they gave him back his eyesight. (He wasn't particularly handsome either, I am told.)

So he loves it when I call myself a midnight girl.

He holds me close and out of habit describes to me the constellation of traditional houses, mixed with chic cafes that serve every possible cuisine and more, the quaint little coffee shops that remind him of the one year we spent in Paris, and also of the few months we spent in Singapore. When we hadn't shifted to Hong Kong, Dad had pitched Hong Kong to me as a gurgling cauldron of cultures and experiences, the consumerism of the chic West embroidered dextrously into the intricate fabric of the East, hoping that I would play along, not knowing that I trusted him more than myself.

'We have been on this escalator forever!' I exclaim.

'It's the longest,' he says. 'And on our left is the first cafe I ever went to in Hong Kong. There are three more that have sprung up near it. I keep seeing construction workers all around, but I can never see what they build, but after a few months, a new building or a new restaurant crops up somewhere. The city is constantly rebuilding itself!'

'It's so different when Deep describes it to me,' I say. 'He makes it sound more like people, souls, birds and happiness, and you make it sound like bricks and mortar.'

'That's the difference between men and *young men*.'

'Aw! Are you jealous? You don't have to be, because I love you more!' I clutch his arm tighter.

'*More*? Which means . . .?'

'Oh, shut up!' I say. 'You're as much a man as a high-school girl on a sugar rush.'

He laughs.

We are sitting in a French restaurant. We picked it when Dad turned me around, asked me to point to a restaurant randomly, just to prove that we are surrounded by places to eat, each with more tantalizing smells than the other. I have been to a few cities and Hong Kong, by far, smells the most exotic. Maybe it's because every corner treats you to a new cuisine, surprising your senses, playing with your gastronomical needs or because here they take food more seriously than anything else, but like they often say, it's truly the culinary capital. It sure smells like one. The SoHo district, a place I had heard a lot about but have come to just twice is a shocker when it comes to food smells, because of the inexhaustible variety of places to eat.

As Dad and I entered the street, I was at a loss to decide which restaurant smelled better.

'So I can't describe it like your new boyfriend does,' he says, 'but it's really classy with dark wood furniture and the racks after racks of wine and my T-shirt is out of place in this intimate dim-yellow light. I should have worn my suit. People are really dressed up here. We should have gone to the pizza place next to this. It is livelier. I think I saw people on a karaoke machine there.'

'You'll be fine. I have never heard anybody not say how gorgeous you look,' I say.

And then he describes and counts at least ten other exotic restaurants he can see from where he's sitting, serving authentic Chinese fare to Indian food to Mexican, places where people are dressed less fancily. He says that we should come here more often, for the SoHo district is really the place to go after a long, hard day at work. 'You have had a pretty stressful day, haven't you?' he nudges naughtily. I chuckle.

I can feel the relaxed atmosphere around me; soft music is piping over the speakers and people's voices are cheerful and devoid of any stress. It sounds and smells like a nice place to be in.

He orders for things that sound suitably French, which he does to impress me, because he knows French cuisine is not my strong point, and I know he's getting a little possessive about me.

He orders for wine, which is another new development, and it means he's really happy today. The food arrives before time and it smells delicious and very French.

'Dad, how do you know so much about French cuisine?' I ask him.

'I was in France for a few meetings for the Indian Air Force. I was young and I wanted to try out everything. The food was free for us, so I hogged like a pig, trying practically everything that came my way,' he explains. 'That was also the time when I bumped into your mom at the Indian airport. She was such a mess when we first met . . .'

When he mentions Mom I know that the topic of discussion has changed. As the wine kicks in, he tells me the story again with moist eyes. A story that becomes more romantic every time he narrates it. Mom fled Afghanistan at the peak of the Soviet-Afghan war, lived in Pakistan for a few months and then flew to India, hoping to forget the devastating war, the loss of her family and start anew. He tells me I have her eyes, a changing shade of green and blue, her honey skin and golden brown hair.

'I was in love the moment I saw her,' he says. 'Plus in those days you didn't really get too much time to fall in love. I chose instantly.'

Dad tells me how he followed her out of the airport and saw her wait for someone who didn't turn up. After an hour he approached her; she hated him at first because he was in his uniform and she had seen enough of war and soldiers, but then trusted him for the same. He gave her his number, and you know, he's kind of charming and chivalrous in a way that only uniformed men can be, so Mom fell for Dad who had already imagined having kids (Yay! Me!) with her.

'Didn't her being a Muslim affect Dada and Dadi?' I ask again because I love how my father turns to mush when he talks about how beautiful Mom was and adds more colours to my painting of her.

'You think? My mother showed off your mom to everyone in the neighbourhood. She always used to say I didn't deserve her,' he says. 'She was incredible. I miss her so much . . .'His voice is choking and he sounds like he is on the verge of tears, his machismo melting for the second time tonight, and I feel sorry for him. I reach for his hand and he holds it, takes it to his face and kisses it.

'I'm sure she misses you,' I say. 'And me!'

'I'm sure she does. I used to envy how much attention she gave you, and that's even before you became a Daredevil.'

'Midnight Girl.'

'Yes, that.'

We laugh. He laughs harder because he's drunk.

# 18

I'm not sure how many courses a French dinner has, but I'm sure it's our fiftieth. Dad's positively drunk, so he's shouting over the din of the restaurant, which is now packed. Halfway through my chocolate cake, I hear someone call out Dad's name.

'RANBEER!'

There is the sound of shuffling feet, followed by the unmistakeable sound of bodies hugging each other.

'What are you doing here?'

'I'm on a date with my daughter! It's her birthday,' he says excitedly.

'You must be Ahana. Happy Birthday, darling,' the lady says and I like that she doesn't shout the words. Usually, people tend to shout the first time they talk to me, like I'm deaf too. She says, 'I'm Sadhika. I work with your dad.'

'Hi, Sadhika and thank you,' I say.

'You're so beautiful!' she remarks and I blush, although I have no real concept of beauty. All I know is that Mom was beautiful.

'Thank you.'

'Why don't you join our table?' Dad asks her.

'I wouldn't want to impose,' she says but Dad cuts her off. She joins us at our table.

They start talking about office, work, Sadhika's son Varun, the next projects, while I devour the chocolate cake. Her words are measured, delivered with confidence, yet when she talks about India and her son, there is a softness, a vulnerability, like whipped cream. I listen to their conversation in snippets, Dad asking all the right questions, acknowledging the silences, supporting her statements and standing by her beliefs; Dad's such a player! I smile to myself at the thought.

'Your father is a great pilot,' Sadhika suddenly says to me.

'Huh? Do you want some cake?' I say as a reflex, guilty for having finished it. 'Oh, him?'

'Yes. He's brilliant. He's a little reckless for he thinks of himself as Tom Cruise from *Top Gun* and gives all the engineers in the box nightmares, but otherwise he's great. He's a big hit with the ladies as well!' she says. 'Did he tell you about Jessica? Oh, and Connelly? The women in our office love him, especially when he comes to office riding his Harley.'

'My dad can be such a wannabe sometimes. I'm sure women love him, but he's taken. He has a full-time job attending to me,' I remark.

'You're a grown-up girl. Cut your dad some slack. He needs to date, too,' she laughs.

I like her. She's not treating me like a disabled person. In fact, I think she just, kind of, borderline, made fun of it.

'I'm not sure what to say here,' Dad says. 'But if Ahana allows me, I can sure ask you for a dance.'

There is silence and I feel two pairs of eyes turn towards me and I nod.

'I will be back,' he whispers in my ear and kisses it.

Chairs are pulled back, there is shifting of feet, Sadhika runs her hands through my hair, about which I should be appalled but I'm not, and I order a cheesecake.

They dance to a couple of songs and return to the table. It's time for us to leave. Sadhika wishes me goodnight and kisses me on my cheek, which I don't mind, before telling me that I have the most beautiful eyes, which doesn't sound affected. She hugs me, tells me that she always wanted a daughter and would love to take me out shopping some time. I nod happily.

Although Dad's unsteady himself, he is holding my hand, and we are back in the never-ending escalator.

'Did you have fun tonight, Dad?'

'Me? Yes. Did you? Sadhika is kind of nice, isn't she?' he asks.

'Yes, I'm sure she's one of the ladies in the office who really like you,' I mock.

'It's nothing like that,' he brushes it aside. 'It's just that she's a little lonely after her divorce from her asshole of a husband. She's too brainy for me anyway. I'm a retired soldier and she's an aeronautical engineer with PhDs in something that enables her to make aircrafts fly.'

'That sounds like the perfect love story, Dad. Brainy, geeky, misunderstood single-mom falls in love with a bad-boy pilot who rides around in a Harley with a leather jacket slung across his shoulder,' I respond.

'You're spending way too much time with your writer boy,' he says.

'Don't change the topic,' I say. 'I like her. She's really nice. She didn't once mention my disability, treated me nicely and sounded really genuine. You need adult friends. I know I'm kind of awesome, but still.'

'I will think about it,' he answers.

'How does she look?' I ask.

'Smashing.'

19

On some days shit just hits the fan and I'm a mess. Today is one of those days. I wake up in total darkness, which is okay considering it's almost always dark for me. I claw myself from under the soft duvet, yawn, and wish Dad would be around but he's not here. He's at work for there is money to be earned, women to be wooed and aircraft to be tested.

I just feel sad and alone.

My mouth tastes stale, so I walk to the washroom, but not before I stub my toes twice because despite my condition, my direction sense is just awful. It's so quiet today. There are no families outside gearing up for their day of sightseeing in Hong Kong, the hotel staff is not creating a ruckus to ensure every room is clean as if it's a hospital, and in general, it's borderline depressing. I just want to crawl up in my bed again with a tub of ice cream, listen to a few movies, and cry.

But before I can order the ice cream, I'm already in bed, crying. Being a brave girl with a disability is okay, coping up and living life to the fullest despite the circumstances is great, but all I really want on days like this is to be a normal girl. Not brave, not courageous, just a girl who can have a lot of friends, doesn't have to be a pain in her father's ass, and can look at her own face in the mirror. I wish to be like others, fall in love, hold someone's hand not because I have to, but because I want to; a normal life where I can grow old with someone, have a few kids I can see playing, and maybe pet another dog who doesn't get run over.

But I'm crying not because it's all pent up in me and today's the day when it's got to erupt, but because these small eruptions are generally good for releasing steam. At least that's how I feel after the overwhelming and all-consuming feeling of misery passes. But while it's still happening, like right now, I just feel twenty shades of pathetic.

It's like things go the way they go every day. Life follows the same routine—I wake up to nothing new or exciting. Every day is the same. Except some days, days like today, when I wake up with a powerful desire of going right back to sleep. And maybe be spared the pain of ever having to wake up again. I'm just tired, tired of the monotony, tired of pitying myself and my dad, tired of being the subject of sympathy for everybody who crosses my path, and of being so pathetically obsessed with a guy who doesn't give a shit about me. There, I said it, he might be cruel, he might be insensitive, but I really, *really* like Aveek. Still.

I wish I had joined college this year, and not put it off until next year. But I was too scared of finding myself in a regular college. Going to school-for-kids-with-special-needs was fine, but going to a college with students who aren't suffering from what I am scares me.

Now all I can have is being left at a hotel room, with nothing but a piano, an instrument I'm not even very good at playing. I have all this fancy stuff made for 'special' people like us. Movies that I can hear, video games that don't have videos and are custom-designed for people like me, audio books, music and . . . well, that's it.

I once had this fleeting affair with working out, which was cut short after just a week because the treadmill Dad bought for me was a regular treadmill, and even though I had tried very hard to remember which buttons to press to START and STOP, I ended up setting it on a speed too high, and it got difficult to breathe, and I searched frantically for the STOP button, but couldn't. Ultimately, my legs gave up and I collapsed on the conveyor belt and was thrown off. Dad, who came running out of the washroom where he was getting ready for office decided it best to take the treadmill back to the store and not let me near anything that operates on power without supervision. I don't know how Aveek does it. Oh yes, it's his stupid clicks.

I hate everything today. I hate Dad's optimism like Aveek does. If only he accepted the fact that there will be no miracle, scientific or otherwise, and I will never be able to see again, and I will be a blind kid in a regular college.

My thoughts come back to my current state. Company— maybe that's what I need. Like every self-respecting brave girl who has ever faced depression, I, too, do the obvious and call my ex-boyfriend, who says I often cry without reason, which is true but he doesn't have to say it.

'Are you still in town?' I ask him.

'Yes, I am. I'm here for the next two weeks. What happened?' he asks. He's making his famed clicking sounds. And for a minute, all I can think of is how good things were between us, before they got bad.

When I met Aveek, it was the first time I had connected with somebody other than my dad. I felt this instant bond between us, like this was meant to be, like it was destiny and we were going to be together forever. We could talk about anything under the sun, and I felt like he actually *understood*. People like us aren't usually supposed to fall in love, or find someone whom we can spend our lives with, but when he came along, I thought it would change, I thought I was the lucky one!

Of course, I wasn't the lucky one, the turn of events eventually revealed that the feeling was not all that mutual, and all the emotions I had felt were probably because I missed my friends, all of whom I had to leave behind because Dad and I were nomads, shifting from city to city, from one special school to another. But the first few months . . . those were something.

'I was just a little bored sitting in my room. I was wondering if you could come over for a while. We can talk and stuff,' I suggest.

'Oh. Fine, I will! Your dad isn't there, is he?' he asks. 'I don't want to get into an argument with him again. He pisses me off.'

'He isn't here,' I respond. It really bugs me when he says bad things about my dad, but right now, I don't care. I miss him and I want him here, with me. I need to feel loved and desired, and may be kissing Aveek and letting him grope me a little would make me feel a little wanted.

Aveek agrees to come over in thirty minutes and I push myself off the bed, to the washroom. I want to be ready for him. Looking good is pointless, but the senses of smell, touch, taste and hearing will be in play and I need to make the best of it. I rummage through the bars of assorted heart-shaped soaps in the basket and pick up each of them to smell. I finally settle on one that smells like oranges, because I remember him telling me once that he likes oranges. After my shower, I brush my teeth again, this time with extra care. I smear plum-flavoured body lotion over myself and pick out a pair of shorts and a T-shirt to wear. I shuffle though my iPod to select music. Smell—check; orange-scented soap would do the trick. Touch—check; plum body milk. Taste—check; fresh mint toothpaste and chocolate lip balm. Hearing—almost check; I don't know if he'll like Enrique, or if anyone listens to him any more. But I know Aveek listens to hard metal, which isn't really appropriate for the kind of mood I'm trying to set here. So Enrique will have to do.

I sit at the edge of my bed and wait. I'm already a little disgusted with myself. It's been forty minutes since he said he'd drop by in thirty, but that's him—always fashionably late. I wonder if he would even care about all the trouble I went through, getting ready for him. There are only two compliments he has ever given me. 1) You're so short, like a bunny. 2) Your err . . . err . . . boobs are soft. The second was more of a universal statement applicable to every second person, ever. So, I'm short for him. That's reassuring.

I sit waiting for him, already feeling all my efforts have gone to waste. I'm bored. I woke up today, depressed and sad, with a slight interest in getting fondled by a guy I'm not sure I like, though I was sure I loved at some point in time, a little bit for sure, but I don't understand why I can't get over my pointless obsession for him. He obviously doesn't care about me, and I am just trying to recreate those first few magical months I had spent with him. But then, that's the thing with obsession—you can't get over it.

I am lying on my bed, flat on my back, as Enrique's voice tries to convince me that he can be my hero, when the doorbell rings. It's been twelve songs, that's roughly forty-five minutes, plus the forty minutes I spent getting ready. He's more than an hour late, and still, the idiot that I am, I jump excitedly from the bed and make my way to the door, measuring my steps.

'Hi, Aveek!' I say as I swing the door open and he barges in. He has this aura around him, which says I-own-everything and I feel it instantly.

'Hi, Ahana. So, you wanted to talk? Let's *talk*,' he says suggestively.

And even though he's reading the signals I sent him, the way he says 'talk' annoys me. It strikes me that instant that he's nothing but a high-headed, self-centred jerk and he'll always be that. It's irritating, but I think it comes with the responsibility of being the golden boy of people with special needs.

I sit down on the bed and he comes to sit next to me. He smells of new furniture and I wonder if he has noticed how I smell yet and if he even likes the smell of oranges, mixed with plum and mint toothpaste and chocolate. He puts his arm around me, which feels like a log of wood, hard and unmalleable—unyielding. I again think of how different he is in my imagination and in reality.

'Romantic music, huh?' he says.

'Yeah, I like Enrique!' I say, a little defensive, a little embarrassed at him pointing out my intentions to seduce him into my life again. I don't feel so good now.

'That's so you,' he says and with his arm around me, he pulls me towards himself and kisses me on the cheek. Once.

Twice. Thrice. And then he starts to kiss my ear, slowly moving down to my neck. Pulling back, he whispers, 'Mmm, you smell good.'

My heart leaps, *he's noticed!* But soon I feel it could be that he is making fun of me by pointing out things I have done to seduce him into this. A part of me wants him gone. Then the thought of being alone in my misery takes over. I just can't stand that right now. Before this irritating confusion eats away more of my mind, I pull him towards me and kiss him on the lips. There. That should keep all other thoughts away.

It still feels forced and unhygienic.

'Whoa!' he says, before starting to kiss me back. He kisses me expertly on the lips, slowly at first and then with more pressure, using both his hands to hold my face in place. I am taken back to our first kiss, the slobbering pointless devoid-of-passion kiss, but I remember how much I was in love with him.

'You really want me, don't you?' he smirks, his fingers slipping from my face to my neck and staying there. In a moment of sudden clarity, I know that I don't want this. I know where this is going and I'm sure I don't want this, so I mumble, 'Stop.' And he thinks I'm being coy like heroines in films where NO means YES, so he nibbles at my ear some more, making it wet, which feels dirty. But surprisingly, also good.

'Ohh. Ohh. Ohh . . .' These are his mating cries, not really sexy. He's still nibbling my ear, his arms are around my neck and we are half on the bed, lying down, but our feet are on the ground.

'Hey, we should stop,' I say, but he ignores my words and kisses me on my lips. He tries to pry them open, using his tongue, but I don't let him.

'Oh, c'mon!' he says a bit frustrated.

'I don't think I want this!' I say and squeeze out of his embrace and sit up. 'We aren't even dating any more!' Which I know is a lame excuse, but I know that if I go on with this, I'll curse myself later for giving in. He doesn't have feelings for me, and if we make out, we would be doing so for all the wrong reasons, and I don't want that.

'I really want to kiss you,' he says.

'We broke up. I don't want to get back into this. It was hard the last time . . .' I say the last part softly, recalling the first few days after the break-up, which felt like someone had ripped a part of me away, and I kept missing that part until I eventually got used to it.

'I really want to kiss you.'

'Please don't,' I say.

'But I do really want to kiss you!' he repeats, with a sense of entitlement. Like I should make myself available because he wants me. This irritates the hell out of me.

'Please!' I say a bit rudely.

'What the fuck, Ahana? You call me early in the morning and ask me to come over to your room. I know that you want me with the way you've dressed up and then I find that you don't even want to kiss me? This is not happening! I left everything and came to you,' he growls.

He's pacing around the room, panting. I wasn't sure about my intention in the morning, a part of me wanted this terribly, another part was staunchly against it, but now his presence has confirmed it for me. There's no more confusion.

'I don't want this,' I say, this time more surely.

'Well, please talk to me when you know what you want!' He almost spits in anger. 'You broke up with me and I said nothing and now you call me over and decide you don't want it. This is just stupid! You're just like your dad!' he shouts.

'Don't bring my dad into this!' I snap angrily.

'Okay, fine. Let's talk about you then. What the fuck do you want? Huh?'

'I don't know! But it's not *this*,' I say, waving my arms wildly around, motioning towards the end of the bed where we were making out just moments ago. As if he can see.

'Oh, yeah? Is that why you called me to your room when you're alone? And put on that perfume? And played that horrible music? Because you did not want to make out?'

'For your information, I'm not wearing any perfume!' I shout back. Somehow, of all the things in the world that I could say, this is the one sentence that escapes my mouth.

'Whatever! You can't waste *my* time like this. I know you don't have anything worthwhile to do, but I do have a life.'

'That's mean. Why are you being so mean?' I break down at his callousness. I'm crying and I hate myself for it. I can never stand up to him and that's why he never respects me.

'Argh. Come on. Not the crying again. It's irritating.'

'Okay, sorry,' I sniff and wipe my tears.

There is silence, and I wonder for a moment if he has left, but then he holds my hand and pulls me into his embrace. He's mumbling *I'm sorry, I'm sorry, I'm sorry* into my ear, and my heart slows down. I forgive him, for it's not only his fault, it's mine too, for maybe I'm difficult and cranky. He's not mad, and neither am I, he's holding me, he cares about me, he loves me.

I wrap my arms around his neck and rub my face against his chest. He bends down slightly to kiss my forehead and it feels alright. His hands pat my back reassuringly, and then they slip inside my T-shirt, flapping around to reach for the hook.

I stagger back. *What is happening?*

I push him away. He tries to grab me again and I slap his hands away.

'What now?' he asks, clearly irritated.

'Get out!' I reply through clenched teeth.

'What?'

'You heard me.'

'Are you kidding me?' he asks. I'm appalled. He just said he was sorry and then tried to feel me up again. What's wrong with him? What's wrong with *me*?

'Just go away and never come back. YOU HEAR ME? I DON'T WANT YOUR ARROGANT ASS AROUND ME ANY MORE!'

'Hey, stop shouti—'

'Or WHAT? WHAT WOULD YOU DO, HUH? SOMETHING WORSE THAN YOU ALREADY HAVE? Just get the hell out of here, you narcissistic, selfish bastard. I have had enough of this shit and I'm not taking any more of it. I always thought deep down you're a good person, but I now know that Dad was right.'

'Your dad is an asshole—'

'DON'T YOU DARE!' I thunder. I'm not going to hear one bad word about my dad from him any more. I take two quick steps towards him, my otherwise weak senses working double-time, and grab his collar, pulling his face towards mine. And then, I say slowly, my jaws tight, measuring my words, 'Don't. You. Ever. Say. Anything. About. My. Dad.'

He pulls himself back and mumbles, 'Whatever,' before he starts to make those clicking sounds again. A second later, I hear the door being shut.

Now, he's gone. And I'm alone again. Before he came

over, I was alone, but at least I had the hope of reclaiming lost love. Now I don't even have that.

I'm standing frozen at my spot, crying, when the door opens again.

'Ahana?' Deep's cracking, unsure voice says.

'Deep? What are you doing here?' I panic.

'I . . . uh, I'm sorry. I heard raised voices . . . so . . .'

'So what?' I snap, because I'm mad at Aveek and irritated at the entire world and embarrassed because I still feel naked and exposed. 'It's none of your business.'

'I just . . . I thought . . .' Deep stammers.

'What? What did you think? If you have a loud noise complaint, go to the reception!'

'No! I just . . . wanted to make sure you're okay . . .'

'WHY? BECAUSE YOU CARE SO MUCH ABOUT THE PATHETIC BLIND GIRL NEXT DOOR? BECAUSE YOU PITY ME? I DON'T NEED NO ONE'S PITY,' I scream.

'It's not that . . . I care about—' Deep tries again, but I cut him off harshly.

'BULLSHIT. Don't you give me that! Why would you care? You are a normal guy, smart enough to get a paid scholarship to this project overseas, with a life waiting for you once you get back home. Why do you care? You're just a tourist!'

'Ahana, don't say that. I do—'

'No, you DON'T. YOU DON'T, YOU DON'T, YOU DON'T. And don't try to convince me otherwise, because YOU DON'T.'

There is a brief silence, during which I hear my own rough, heavy breathing. And then I hear Deep mutter, 'Sorry,' really softly, and leave, shutting the door behind him.

And in that very second, my knees give way and I fall to the floor, big tears falling down my cheeks. I cry and I cry and I cry.

I lost all track of time as I lay on the floor, curled into a ball and wept. But when I finally sit up and wipe my tears and brush my hair back behind my ears, I feel raw. My upper lip seems a little swollen and it aches to open my eyes.

I wash my face, curse myself for what I said to Deep, gulp down a glass of water, curse myself for what I should have said to Aveek long ago, grab my cell phone, shove it into my handbag and walk slowly out of my room, locking the door behind me. I walk for ten feet and knock. When the door opens up, I hear my broken voice say, 'Deep, can you please take me to Disneyland?'

20

We are on the Disneyland resort line of the Hong Kong subway, which Deep tells me, is pretty and has windows shaped like Mickey Mouse. He's holding my hand. I'm listening to him, sometimes crying, sometimes blowing my nose—in general, a mess.

'We are here,' he says, and leads me out of the Metro station. He has conveniently ignored that I'm crying and hasn't once asked why I was in tears, or mentioned my outburst. Instead he told me I looked quite remarkable even with a running nose

Deep is quite kicked about our trip and finds it difficult to believe they actually built a part of the Metro to specifically take people to Disneyland.

'It's like the cupboard of Narnia,' he had said. 'If you feel stressed, you just have to take the Metro and you reach here—in DISNEYfreakingLAND!'

We walk out of the Metro station, through the gigantic gate which Deep tells me says Disneyland in a million different colours, to the fountain with Mickey Mouse surfing on the top of it. I distinctly remember how Mickey Mouse looks because he was on the first bag I carried to school. I had picked up that one myself, rummaging through bags featuring Pluto and Minnie Mouse and Donald Duck. I tell Deep about my first day in school, about how happy I was, and he tells me he had cried himself hoarse and had to be dragged to the classroom.

'Aw! There are little kids dressed as fairies and Cinderellas and Sleeping Beauties. We should totally get you into one of those. This is *amazing*,' he says.

'You wish,' I say. 'Thank you for coming.'

'Thank you for inviting me or I would have spent another day watching English movies dubbed in Mandarin,' he says. He asks me if I want a year-long ticket, with multiple entries to Disneylands across countries, and I say he would not be around every time to go with me, so what's the point!

After we are frisked, he gets his hands on what he likes best—a map. We walk arm in arm, because he's engrossed in the map, figuring out the game plan to tackle the 'sprawling' (as he puts it) amusement park. He suggests that we walk around the entire area to see what's in store, and he doesn't stop talking, which is great because I'm in no mood to talk.

He tells me that the entrance to the park is fashioned on a street in Texas of the 1800s, lined with shops that look exactly like the ones he has seen in the movies. They are selling stuffed toys and Disney merchandise, but could have very well been selling horse hooves and guns. 'I'm sure they shoot movies here!' he says, 'No one would know it's 2013!'

He drags me to Toy Story Land, where he clicks pictures of us with Buzz Lightyear and Woody. He buys me a pizza, that's in a cone, and it gives me some strength, because right now I'm out of energy to keep up with a six-year-old Deep.

He's almost running as he drags me to Grizzly Gulch, which he tells me is a to-the-scale reconstruction of an old mine, and that he will have nightmares about it. 'The bears are real . . . no they are not,' he says, almost shocked. 'Look! There's a jail!' he says and runs to it. I'm panting, trying to keep up with his pace, also because his enthusiasm is infectious. He's running, touching everything he can, clicking pictures like he's a Nat Geo photographer and this is a rare sighting of a woolly mammoth. And just when I'm about to tell him that, he drags me to the Adventure Land, which sounds extra creepy since it's a recreation of a rainforest. When I ask him if it's scary to look at, he just tells me, 'It could very well have been real.'

'Oh shit. Two hours gone! . . . We need to get on some rides, too . . . Shit, this place is so big! We will go to the Space Mountain first! It promises an adventurous ride through the galaxies of space, which would unravel the secrets of the stars and the nebulas,' he reads from the map. 'We can't miss out on that!' he says excitedly.

Coming to Disneyland was my defence against depression, but now it seems like we are here for him! He's walking way faster than he usually does. He keeps getting hold of people, asking them to click pictures of us in crazy caps made of Disney characters. He tells me he would take entire shops of stuffed toys and remote-controlled cars home if he could.

'Whatever you say, captain!' I respond.

'I'm so happy you got me here. This is like another world. If someone asks me what my heaven should look like, it should be this. Pizza cones and space rides and Buzz Lightyear,' he mumbles as we stand in the line to unravel the secrets of the universe on an indoor roller coaster. Then he whispers, 'When you had first said *take me to Disneyland*, I'd thought it had a sexual connotation.'

'Did you Google?'

'What else would I do?' he says. 'I'm a novice in all matters regarding the opposite sex.'

'I don't believe you. You're quite the charmer.'

'I'm a bundle of awkwardness. Apart from yours and my first girlfriend's, whom I don't think I liked very much, the only hand I have held is my mother's, and though it feels great, it is nothing like this,' he says it casually, like I will not hyperventilate.

'What does this feel like?' I ask.

'Our ride is here,' he says, avoiding my question. We step into a make-believe spaceship, ready for the ride that will change the way we or rather he looks at space, forever. I'm glad he didn't answer because right now, I really want to be kissed.

Roller coasters are scary. We have been on three of them already, each one scarier than the previous one; Deep keeps assuring me *It will be okay*, though I'm more bothered when he breathes into my ear while saying it. This is the most fun I have had in the longest time; it's the best sounding place I have ever been to—it sounds like gushing water, and wind blowing through trees, and the best parts of the music of the cartoon films I have listened to as a child and as a grown-up.

We are eating Indian food today because he got really excited when he saw an outlet selling Indian thalis, and I can hear him chew his food down enthusiastically, which is probably the only unattractive thing about him.

'Deep? Can I ask you something?'

'Sure,' he mumbles from under the relentless, almost vicious, munching.

'How do you look?' I ask. 'Not that it matters, but you know, just like that. I'm curious.'

'Didn't your dad tell you?'

'As a person who goes by what people tell her, I have noticed that guys don't describe other guys very well. Dad only describes other men as *he's okay* or *he isn't nice*. You're okay.'

'Thank God!' he responds. 'If you go by what the current standards for being hot or nice or good-looking are, I'm at the dimmest end of the spectrum. I'm almost embarrassing . . .'

'I'm sure you're not,' she says. 'And even if you are, I don't think it matters. The first thing everyone says about Dad is that he's attractive, which is strange because he's a really nice person and no one talks about that.'

'Your blind wisdom. Just the best.'

'Eyes complicate stuff,' I say.

'Stupid eyes, always ruining everything,' he agrees.

We finish our lunch, walk around the amusement park, and he keeps clicking pictures of me, which no one else has ever done. Except Dad.

'Oh, damn,' he exclaims suddenly. 'Wait here. Don't go anywhere. And if someone grabs you, tell them that you're not a Disney character, although you might be as cute.'

'But—'

He's gone.

And then I feel something soft against my face. Like a snout. With fur.

'What's it?' I ask.

'I found your exact replica. The first time I saw you, I remember thinking to myself that you're like a stuffed toy, but out of production. But I found you here. You're the inspiration behind . . . LOLA! This yellow-coloured bundle of joy. Look at her, I mean touch her, she's exactly like you,' he says excitedly.

'You have lost it, Deep! Have you been drinking?' I ask, steeling myself, to hide that inside I'm mush, I'm melting.

'I'm sorry. But she really does look like you,' he insists.

'You're such a kid,' I say, still not ready to give into his sweet talk, because if I do, I'm going to grope him and eat him up.

'I just love Disney characters!' he defends himself and it's so cute that I throw myself at him and hug him and mumble 'That's so cute!'

'Who's Lola, by the way?' I ask, caressing the stuffed toy, which has big eyes and a round bottom, in my hand.

'Bugs Bunny's girlfriend,' he says. 'I used to be an authority on Disney characters till the time Dragon Z came and spoiled it all.'

He leads me to other rides, some of which involve getting on a boat and finding ourselves in the middle of a fake tropical rainforest which sounds very real. He makes me pose for pictures wearing headgear inspired from all things Disney.

'Are you Bugs Bunny?' I wanted to ask him.

# 21

I literally had to drag Deep out of Disneyland. By the end of it, I was sure he wanted to get himself an Aladdin costume and dress me up like Minnie Mouse.

'I have no intention of going back to watching television again,' he says. He's had too much cotton candy.

'We are not going back to the hotel. We are just going some place quieter,' I say. 'Find the bus terminal on the map and look for the bus that goes to Tai O.'

'Tai O?' he repeats after me and I hear him shuffling to check his map. He's good at this stuff. Also at holding hands, and making me feel like a cute Disney character. That also makes me wonder how good he is at kissing, which I ask him when I get on the bus.

'When was the last time you kissed anybody?' I ask. He falls over me as the bus turns, probably negotiating a sharp turn.

'That would be never,' he says. 'This looks exactly like the road to Shimla or Nainital. Oh, look. This is an entire different island. We were here, on the Hong Kong Island, and now we are on Lantau Island. We will take the ferry back to the hotel.'

He conveniently ignores that I asked him a question and becomes a *Lonely Planet* guide, telling me about the cluster of islands that are collectively called Hong Kong, expressing shock over how we traversed over water in a Metro and we didn't even notice, and how excited he is to go back to the island where our hotel is on a ferry. I tell him that we can also choose to go back to the Hong Kong Island using a cable car which is the longest cable car in Asia and separates one from the water and forests below by just a glass floor, but he's scared and tells me that the ferry's a more romantic option. I try to convince him, since Dad told me the views from the cable car are terrific and terrifying, beautiful and overwhelming, but he says he doesn't take heights very well. As if I didn't remember that from the day we went on the observatory deck.

'You have never kissed anyone?' I ask again.

'I'm saving it for my wife.'

'Are you serious?'

'Of course not, but you made it sound like it's so odd that I haven't kissed anyone. On a scale of 1 to 10 on how kiss-worthy a person is, I am a minus hundred.'

'I don't buy that,' I say and put my head on his shoulder, partly because I'm tired, partly because he's never been kissed, and mostly because he's not holding my hand, I miss his touch.

'How have you been doing in the kissing business?' he asks shyly.

'I have kissed three, and though the quality has been questionable, I think I'm doing okay in terms of quantity,' I declare, wondering if he will think of me as promiscuous and try kissing me, which I totally wouldn't mind.

'When it comes to kissing, quality trumps quantity. That's like the only rule to kissing,' he responds.

'For someone who has not kissed, you sure do know a lot of rules,' I smirk.

'That's how I roll.'

It takes us about an hour to reach Tai O, home to a small fishing community. This is where I first came a year back with Dad and fell in love with the quietness of the place—a far cry from the relentless buzzing activity of the Hong Kong Island.

'Where is the village?' I ask him and he says he'll check the map. We walk around like headless chickens, asking people for directions to the village and when we finally get there, it's familiar once again. The narrow winding lanes with the small houses that Deep describes to me, the sound of wind unhindered by the high-rises, the creaking of small doors, the barking pet dogs, it all comes back to me in a rush of memories.

'Be careful,' Deep says, as he holds my hand tighter and asks me to walk closer to him.

'Where are we?' I ask, a little alarmed. The wind has picked up and it's hitting my face and I can smell the sea.

'Umm, we are literally over the sea, and I'm not misusing the word literally. The village is built over water, and the passageways . . . hey, careful! are leading us from one house to another. I think we just entered someone's house—and there are fishing nets and rusted air-conditioners lying about, also there are like these motor boats tied to the wooden pillars these houses stand on. I'm sure this is someone's home, hey, there's a dog there! It's so quiet and so beautiful. I think the bus just dropped us to the 1800s. It's like Venice made out of wood. Truly, it is the Venice of the Orient,' he says, 'let's just sit here.'

He makes me sit with my legs dangling over the edge and tells me that we could be sitting on someone's veranda, but as he notes from the guide book that he has been reading, people in the Tai O village community don't mind mingling, and often passageways pass through living rooms.

'The sun's setting,' he says. 'The sea is about to swallow the sun only so it can spit it out somewhere else.' Then he puts his hand around my shoulder and I snuggle into his armpit, and it's not weird, just really romantic. Of the few moments that I do feel like seeing, this is one of them. I want to see the sun set, I want to see the small waves Deep describes. I want to watch the village folks immerse themselves in their daily work, fish, sell their produce in the local market, which is flocked by tourists, come back home and live in their tiny huts suspended over the sea. I really want to see.

'Have you been in love?' Deep asks softly, which is really weird because he never says things like this.

'I don't know what love is,' I respond. It's true.

'Ditto. The closest I have ever been in love is with Holly Smale,' he says.

'I thought I was your biggest conquest ever overseas,' I smirk.

'She's a geek turned failed supermodel turned geek author,' he clarifies. 'And you will never be a conquest. I'm like Alexander the Great and you're India. I end with you,' he mumbles.

I'm mush.

We are back on the bus, and while he has dozed off, I'm still thinking of his Alexander the Great analogy. I hate boys for this very reason. They say things in the heat of the moment, oblivious to the fact that they have just created a bunch of cocoons inside our stomachs, which would transform into butterflies every time they talk to us from then onwards.

*I end with you.*

I mean seriously, did he just have to say that? He could have just said, I'm Alexander the Great and you're India. You give me cholera and I go back to Persia and die a slow death while my soldiers mutiny against me. That would have been so much better. I would have been sleeping as well.

He's still asleep when the bus stops and I can hear people walking off the bus.

'Hey, Deep?' I shake him up. 'I think people have got off the bus.'

'Huh?' He wakes up with a start. 'Damn. Was I drooling? Did you see?'

'No.'

'Oh.'

My Alexander the Great, the man who named twenty cities after his name, sleeps with his mouth open, salivating on himself.

'Where are we?' he asks, shocked, and then I feel him pull out his map again. 'Oh no. We took the wrong bus!'

'Where are we?' I ask. I'm lost with a drooling boy, but it feels okay.

'This is Po Lin Monastery and the Giant Buddha,' he tells me. 'Do you want to roam about here? The next bus is in twenty minutes.'

'I would love to!' I say.

A familiar scent engulfs us, reminds me of the incense of the Man Mo temple, and Deep tells me it's much like that, only bigger, the gold and red more pronounced. Through Deep's running commentary I find out that there are flowers arranged in beautiful patterns on the stairs that lead to the main praying area, where gold-coloured statues await us, enclosed in wooden and gold casing. There is a huge bell he wants to ring but says it's written that it is forbidden to do so. He tells me there are little red-coloured cushions we can rest our knees on and pray. It's very quiet and peaceful. Deep's voice comes down to a whisper.

'I don't want to miss this,' he says, and lets go of my hand, which scares me, and adds, 'Let's pray?'

I close my eyes, and start praying, but I'm thinking of him, which makes me feel guilty, but I'm still thinking of him, so I give up and open my eyes and wait for him to finish. Once done, he leads me down the steps of the monastery and tells me that I have to pose again.

'You can't miss clicking a picture in front of these flowers!' he exclaims. 'Your dad will be so happy when he sees this.' He makes me pose on the steps, in front of the monastery, in front of what he describes as a big steel tub—he cannot tell what it is used for—and in front of the twelve fierce warriors who protect the worshippers during the twenty-four hours of the day, each taking two-hour shifts. Very practical gods indeed!

'Do you want to go up?' he asks. 'It's about two hundred stairs. We'll probably miss the next bus, but we can take the one after that.'

'What awaits us on top of the stairs?'

'Precisely what it says here, a very large Buddha. The

biggest I have ever seen really,' he says and adds after a second. 'Also, some statues that are praying.'

'What do we have to lose?'

We start walking up the stairs and it's harder than I imagined it would be. The first fifty stairs were a breeze, but now my breath is laboured, and I attribute it to my utter lack of exercise. I spent the first five years of my life hoisted six feet off the ground, in Dad's arms, and the next thirteen, I have spent constantly sweeping my cane in semi-circles, and I have been told I shouldn't ever be in any kind of hurry. I might do a lot of walking, but most of it is slow and measured, and stairs for me is a death trap.

We take five breaks before we reach there, and I'm tired and exhausted. 'Now what?' I ask.

'We talk to the big guy,' he says.

'You just talked to him downstairs,' I argue.

'This one is a different flavour,' he quips, and quite frankly, I am shocked he remembers what I said that day. But he's right, you have to walk up, get tired, show your commitment to God, to get your wishes fulfilled. It's a lesson for life. Meet people halfway. It's something Dad always tells me.

We sit on the stairs in silence. And then Deep tells me that he can sit there and look at the panoramic view of the Lantau island, green and vast and quaint, for days at end. He tells me it feels like time has stopped at the prettiest moment of all of history. He slips his fingers into mine and it's so beautiful and complete that I want to cry. I just want to cry. I don't know why but I do want to cry.

'What did you say to the big guy?'

'I like his curls,' he says.

'Seriously.'

'I can't tell you what I asked for,' he says. 'It won't come true otherwise.'

'I told you mine.'

'The ones you asked for yourself, not the one you asked for me,' Deep argues.

'You wished something for me?' I ask, positively, happily shocked.

'Who else would I wish for?' he responds.

Deep is my favourite type of boy.

# 22

The ferry pushes off from the harbour, and Deep's jumping on his seat, looking over, and constantly asking me to, '*Look!*' and then apologizing. He tells me there is only water in front of us as far as his eyes can see, and that the million light bulbs of the Hong Kong Island are like twinkling stars in the sky, and how completely immersed in the world he feels while the ferry is cutting through water that is engulfing it completely. 'It's like being lost, yet not so.'

'It all comes together now,' he says, 'the yachts, the smaller vessels, the big tankers, not colliding into each other, but how do you think they managed this in the olden times? It must have been crazy back then!'

I want him to keep talking. He's gone from holding my hand, to caressing it and I just want that to keep going. The ferry feels faster than I thought it would be. I can feel I'm on water, floating, in a transition, going towards land, and hope, and Dad on the other side. Suddenly, it's breezy and I'm cold, and before I can tell him, he wraps an arm around my shoulder. I feel calmed, and a sense of relief flows over me.

'The sun has almost set. The water looks as if embellished

with tiny diamonds. The buildings are still very far away,' he says.

*Any other boy would have just said, 'It's dark, let's go home,'* I think to myself.

I close my eyes and pretend I'm asleep because I want to soak in this moment and not talk. He, too, doesn't say a word for the rest of the ferry ride, except once when he tells me that it's darker now and he can see the lights faraway, that it feels like he and I are the only ones left behind after an apocalypse, and that it feels so right. He says it in the air and I'm not sure if he is speaking to me, but I have goosebumps all over my body.

'We are here,' he says, 'And I think your phone's ringing.'

It's indeed ringing. Even with my supposedly superhuman ears, I couldn't hear it ring. 'Hi, Dad . . . I'm with Deep . . . A little . . . with him? . . . Okay . . . we will take a cab . . . okay.'

'What did he say?' he asks.

'What do you think about having dinner with Dad and a friend of his?'

'That it's scary and I would rather jump into this freezing water and die?'

'He's not that bad! Why do you say that?'

'Because he's perfect and I'm not, because he's handsome and I'm not, and mostly because I want him to think of me as a good boy, and the more I meet him, the more I will be at risk of spoiling my image,' he explains.

'Why do care so much?'

'Because he's your dad,' he answers and shuts me up. We catch a cab and he waits for me to say something.

'We are still going, right?' I ask.

'I would never say no to you.'

I smile. Seriously, this boy has to stop being a male protagonist from a cheesy Nicholas Sparks book.

'Take us to Jordan, Temple Street Night Market.'

When we meet Dad and Sadhika, they are shopping. Deep tells me that both their hands are full of gigantic shopping bags, and they tell us that they are still not done.

'Your Dad is quite the shopper,' Deep says. 'He and his lady friend are devouring every shop. And strangely, your dad is better at the bargaining bit. He's a pro.'

'He took oestrogen shots when Mom died to cope up with my Mom needs.'

'I'm glad he took those. Because right now he's just an old Taylor Lautner, but without those, who knows, he might have been Conan the Barbarian.'

'I need to tell Dad this!'

'If you don't like me, you can just tell me. Why this elaborate ruse to get rid of me?' he asks and we laugh.

He tells me all the stuff Dad's buying, which is embarrassing, and he's scared that the bags Dad's carrying might explode, at which point Dad and Sadhika each buy a suitcase and dump all their items in them and calmly roll on. Deep is appalled at Dad's stamina to shop in a street market, a trait attributed predominantly to young women, but he blames it on the street shops, which are lit up like Christmas tress, much like the rest of Hong Kong, and are selling everything from shoes, umbrellas shaped like guns (which Dad bought), role play costumes that Deep refuses to describe, tiny tea sets, huge tea sets, headphones in a bazillion colours, gambling sets, and Hong Kong T-shirts that say, 'The Wonders Never Cease'. He tells me about the little trinkets, pieces of jewellery, and souvenirs and paintings that the shopkeepers are selling, driving bargains that are quite hard to resist. Deep buys a handbag for his mom at a throwaway price and can't stop telling me about how pretty it is. The street, which is enveloped by these little shops is never-ending and seductive, Deep says, and a sharp contrast to the luxury brands whose showrooms glitter in gold and silver and are lined almost all throughout the landscape of Hong Kong. It's addictive, he adds.

After Dad and Sadhika are done with buying half of Hong Kong and stuffing it into their suitcases, we find ourselves in a restaurant that smells like Japanese—even the waiter addresses us in Japanese.

'So, Deep, how's work?' Dad asks after we are done ordering. I want his questions to be easy to answer for I have learned that Deep is easily thrown off his game by human attention.

'They don't really care if I turn up in office because then they have to deal with what work they have to give me. So it's great!' he replies.

'Deep is here on a software internship project,' Dad explains to Sadhika. 'And she's an aeronautical engineer and builds the planes I fly. She's brilliant!'

'That's so cool,' Deep says. 'I have sold my life to software. We get a lot less credit than we deserve. Like rag-pickers. But I don't mind it all that much.'

Dad and I don't get the joke but Sadhika laughs and says, 'Don't be too hard on yourself. The software industry is probably the only one where you can be seventeen and a millionaire!'

'That only makes it worse,' Deep quips. 'Not that I care too much about being a millionaire, but I wouldn't mind it either.'

'He's a writer,' I interrupt. I know Deep hates it when I say that, but I love the word and I love to think of him as one, so I just keep telling everybody who'd listen.

'Oh, is he? That's interesting,' Sadhika says.

'Writing is for girls,' Dad says and laughs.

'Dad!' I snap. 'You have been lugging a pink suitcase for the past half an hour, shopping like you just won a lottery.'

'Shopping is very manly activity. It's like hunting and gathering, like cavemen, only here you have to pay,' he defends himself.

'You can't get past that,' Sadhika adds. 'I was surprised, too, when I saw him attack those shops with a vengeance.'

We laugh.

We eat prawn rolls, and sushi, and something I don't know the name of, but it tastes delicious. Dad leaves with Sadhika after waving down a cab for Deep and I.

Once I'm back in my room I crash. And this time, I sleep for real.

# Part Three

# Hold My Hand

# 23

Ranbeer wakes up exactly at 5 a.m., like he has done for the past ten years, brushes his teeth and changes into his Aéropostale gym trousers and an Abercrombie & Fitch T-shirt that is a size too small for him. He tiptoes out of the hotel room that he and his daughter share and runs down the eighteen floors to the gym, working up a nice sweat before he starts working out. Today, it's back and legs, his favourite body parts to work on, and he starts with a mix of squats and deadlifts.

Hotel gyms are mostly empty, he has noticed, except for the odd gym rat or the vacationing sports guy or middle-aged women looking for gym trainers to spend some fun time with. He likes it this way. Working out alone gives him plenty of time to think. Today, there is just one woman, in her early thirties he reckons, running furiously on a treadmill, the balls of her feet pounding the belt. It reminds him of how time has passed him by, because only yesterday he could run a mile under four minutes, something that seems out of reach now. He's forty-four, without a wife, without a home to go back to, and a blind daughter whom he loves dearly.

Being a mother to Ahana has been delightful, it's the only

time he doesn't miss Farah, the woman who still has an iron grip on his heart. It's been twelve years since she's been gone. It seems like only yesterday that he followed her around the airport, thinking of what to say to her, and at the same time juggling the possibilities that lay ahead if she was single, wondering if she would be accepted in his family, and making up his mind to fight for her come what may.

Ever since she went, losing her fight to a cancer which no one could detect in time, he has been running from one city to another, looking for respite from thoughts of her, from the life he thought he would have with her, guilty of how weak he felt sometimes, and wrecked because he thought he wasn't being a good father. Farah often used to say that she's married to a teenager, and this wasn't far from the truth. Some men aren't supposed to grow up, and Ranbeer was one of them.

Fatherhood wasn't that hard on him, loving Ahana was his second nature, but nurturing her was Farah's job, and when she died, his world came tumbling down and he was rudderless. And as if that wasn't tough enough, Ahana had gone blind, struck by a congenital disease that affects the optic nerve. This had happened a year before Farah had died, but it was what they saw as a small blip in a long, blissful familial life. They never saw her disability as something that could derail their life; it was just another chore to be taken care of, like the laundry, or the dishes. The cancer, though brief, was fierce and destroyed Farah, who went from being a beautiful woman to being a gaunt, weak cancer victim in a matter of months. It emptied their savings, and destroyed the life they had painstakingly built together.

He left his job and went private, flying planes for corporations that needed trained, courageous pilots who could test new aircraft. The pay was good and he knew it was the only way he could have paid for the special schools that were essential for Ahana to cope with her blindness. Between then and now, they have lived in seven cities. Ahana had grown to be a beautiful woman, uncannily reminiscent of her mother, as if genetics had rejected all his traits.

Ranbeer is in the middle of his leg press drop-set when his phone rings.

'Is it today?' he asks. 'Right now? Fine. I will be there.'

He wraps up his workout with a couple of sets of lunges and back extensions. His flight to New Delhi leaves in two hours, where he is needed to test a new prototype of a small cargo plane that their company has developed. He doesn't want to be late, a habit drilled into him since his days in the Indian Air Force. He runs back to his hotel room, this time his calves are screaming with pain, reminding him that his best days are long gone.

Ahana is still sleeping, curled up in a ball, and looks like a cute puppy wrestling a ball of wool. He washes himself, gets dressed in a T-shirt that says 'LICK', and a pair of faded jeans, and all this while, he can't take his eyes off his daughter, so young, so delicate, so unfortunate, yet so brave.

He goes out of the room to spray himself with cologne, a habit he picked up from experience—Ahana used to wake up due to the smell—and comes back to the room. He kisses her goodbye.

Ranbeer's 1969 Harley Davidson is in its usual spot. He, often begrudgingly, admits he likes the attention he gets when he's on the motorcycle, but maintains it was his love for the bike that made him buy it. He checks his reflection in the rear-view mirror and thinks about Sadhika, the only other woman whom he has let into his life.

It's a fifteen-minute ride but he drives around in circles because he loves to hear the deafening sound of the modified 150cc engine, it makes him the badass of the streets of Hong Kong, but not quite. Years of his daughter's company have made me mellow, like a marshmallow, Sadhika had said.

'Hi, Ranbeer!' Sadhika says and they hug. Just days ago, they were shaking hands, but now they are hugging.

*She's is beautiful, she's broken, she's like me*, he's thinking. His unflinching, unwavering love for Farah never allowed him to be interested in any other woman, although there were always some around, hankering for his attention.

Sadhika was a happily married woman with a young son, until she was not. A long divorce and a messy custody battle had left her thin, fragile and depressed, almost suicidal. He had ignored it at first, the tears, and the disappearances into the Ladies room shortly after every meeting, but then he was reminded of Farah, alone and distressed at the airport, and he wanted to be there for Sadhika.

Their friendship was fuelled by their need to tell someone that life is hard, and no matter how brave a face you put for the world, no matter how much you love your kids, it's always hard bringing them up, and there are days when you wish life were simpler.

'I need you to go through this with me. Also, here's the manual which I want you to read. The aircraft is 456, an upgrade to the 380 we tested a few years back, so I don't want you to ignore the manual. You have four hours on the flight to India. Please put it to good use,' Sadhika instructs like a school teacher. God knows he wanted to hug her and tell her that he needed her, that he understood her pain, and that they could be together.

'What would I do without you?' Ranbeer nods and says—something he has told her a zillion times over the last few years that they have worked together. But usually it was about testing aircraft, while today it was about him. 'I will call you once I land in New Delhi.'

'I will wait,' she answers. 'And please, the manual.'

'Whatever you say, ma'am,' he says and salutes her.

# 24

Deep and Ahana are out in the city again—the city Ahana has come to love more than any other she has lived in. She always knows how the different parts of the city smell like—like Causeway Bay smells like the Times Square in New York or Champs-Élysées in Paris; Tsim Sha Tsui smells like a street in South Delhi; Jordan Street smells like delicious street food and the sweat and happiness of shoppers and shopkeepers alike; and the islands that surround Hong Kong Island, Lantau and Lamma Islands, smell like earth, and quietness and spirituality.

Today, Ahana woke up to her father's call telling her that he wouldn't be home until late night, or probably the next morning, and Deep woke up wondering if it was the right time to call Ahana.

It wasn't until eleven that Ahana called and asked Deep if he could take her to the Hong Kong Museum of Art in Tsim Sha Tsui. She knew Deep was the kind of boy, thoughtful and considerate and intelligent, who would willingly want to go. Deep was kicked about it. The sun was out, so they decided to walk their way to the harbour. Deep had insisted that they would take a ferry again from there, and Ahana liked the idea—the memories of last night's ferry ride were still fresh in her mind.

'Are we there yet?' Ahana asks after some time.

'It's easy to lose yourself in the streets of Hong Kong. But it's not because you don't know your way, it's because the city consumes you in all ways possible,' Deep tells her.

Their fingers are intertwined and though they have been holding hands since the first day that they met, today it feels different. After breaking up with Aveek, Ahana had sworn off boys, she knows she isn't good at dealing with loss. Nothing has been said between Deep and her, and she wants it to remain that way. She wants to believe that she isn't in love with him, that she can let him go and yet get on with her life, but she is having a hard time convincing herself.

Deep hasn't said a word about their relationship either, but she can't blame him. Though she doesn't doubt Deep's affection for her, it can very well be just that—*affection*, not love. It unsettles her how Deep understands her with all her complexities, how he never intentionally brings up her blindness in a conversation, and only thinks of it as a minor quirk, like a sixth thumb, or a purple streak in her hair.

She hates it when he says all the right combinations of words because they stick, and they resonate in her head every night when she goes to sleep. It hurts as much as it feels great because she knows she will never forget the things he has said, and he will. Boys, especially ones with eyes, always forget what they say to girls with no eyes. As Deep puts it, 'Stupid eyes, always ruining everything.' She is surprised how she remembers every conversation she has had with Deep in such detail.

'Oh, there was a shop which looks exactly like a Metro station!' Deep points out.

They have been walking for an hour now, but that's what it's like to walk in Hong Kong. You just want to keep doing it. A five-minute walk turns to an hour and an hour turns into two and then it's already evening. No wonder there are so many foot massage centres in the city, Deep thinks. The roads turn at perfect right angles and they never seem to end. They are just stuck, wilfully, in a never-ending maze with fascinating people and places and shops and temples tucked away in corners.

'Where are we?' Ahana asks.

'We are under a flyover where ten old women are beating something with the soles of their shoes. I read about it online. You give them a reason or a cause for your sorrow and they beat their shoes and it's all gone!' he says, trying to sound excited.

It's been like that all these days. Deep has tried hard to keep Ahana entertained, scared that she might not call, petrified that she might choose Aveek over him and go to some blind convention rather than take him around the city. So whenever he tells her about the goldfish market in Kowloon Island where there are forty-odd shops that sell goldfish in tiny little transparent packets filled with water, making the entire street look like it is water and gold, he hopes she will be fascinated. Or when he makes her smell every one of the zillion flowers that the flower markets have in every conceivable colour, he tries to make it sound like Hogwarts, like they are in a magical place, and strangely enough, he begins to believe his own words.

When he recollects his day at night, thinking of what they

did together, it seems like they walked hand in hand through a land where goldfish swam between big flowers along with ferries that sailed into the sunset—unbelievable and beautiful.

Deep has never felt sorry for Ahana or her disability, for if she were able to see, she would never be with him, and worse, he feared it would change her. He had not yet written a word of his book after the first two paragraphs. It's not that he hadn't tried, but writing didn't come naturally to him, and even when it did, it came in short bursts. The words he wrote could never do justice to Ahana. It was like falling short of words describing your favourite book; you can't explain to another person how much you like it.

They take the ferry again, and he is excited, though not as much as he was the night before. The sun is shining and he's not as brave to caress her hand while she's still awake. They reach the harbour. Deep spots a few couples dressed in flowing white dresses and tuxedos getting their pictures clicked by a professional photographer who continuously suggests new poses. He describes it to her, scared that he wouldn't be able to put in words—the beauty of the moment, the smiles of the couples, their embarrassment and their happiness. The realization that he will never be good enough for her strikes him again.

Being a midnight girl doesn't take away the fact that Ahana, too, is a girl, and she, too, has dreams of being swept off her feet, led to the altar by her father and be married to someone who will always be with her in thick and thin.

And in blindness.

When Deep tells her about the happy couples, painting a picture in front of her, she curses her disability, something she does rarely. Who would want her? She asks herself. She knows Deep romanticizes the smallest of incidents, making them grand and beautiful. Now, she can't help but think of who Deep is thinking about while he describes the whiteness of the brides' dresses. It's definitely not her. Who would want her? She asks herself again.

'Do you know who Andy Warhol was?' Deep asks and she shakes her head, feeling inadequate and stupid. 'He was the pioneer of pop art. I'm not sure what that is, but it's basically people's pictures in different colours. So Marilyn Monroe's is one of the most famous portraits made by him.'

'Why are you telling me all this?' she asks.

'Because you wanted to come to the museum and they have a special exhibition on Andy Warhol. I thought that's why you wanted to come here,' he explains.

'Right.'

She feels small and foolish. This morning, she had turned on the television and had heard someone talk about the museum and she thought it would be a nice pretext to go out with Deep again, but Deep, who knows everything unnecessary, didn't see through it.

They walk around the museum listlessly. Deep tells Ahana about Hong Kong's obsession with preserving history, naming sites as heritage sites all over the city, and restoring them to their past glory. He tells her about the walled villages in Hong Kong like Tsang Tai Uk, amongst scores of others, some of them dating back two hundred years, that their government have now restored. This fossilizing their past—the old houses, the sources of livelihood, the tiny beds, the little walls that protected them—are all for their future to see. He says he has read about them on the Internet and really wants to go, but Ahana is barely listening. It's not the first time Deep has expressed his shock over how the region is furiously building skyscrapers, yet industriously protecting its earthly past, and how this marriage of development and history is seamless and unobtrusive.

Deep buys Ahana a pair of headphones and an audio guide that explains all the artefacts. Ahana can't concentrate at all, and waits for those times when he leans towards her, his face barely inches away and tries to listen in with her. Though it all seems futile to her; eventually Deep has to go, to his world where he has friends and books and family and girls with eyes to date, and she will be alone with only her dad.

She has to let go, she decides.

Deep is no longer interested in seeing paintings on display, yet he keeps bending over so that he can be close to her beautiful face. He notices her expressionless face and stays quiet, letting her concentrate on the audio book while he wallows in self-pity.

The last few days have been so perfect! It's become hard for him to imagine what it would be like not to hold her hand, or not to describe in elaborate detail what's around him. He will miss all this and he wonders if she will too.

Their worlds are different, and although he wants to sit her down and tell her what she means to him, he doesn't have the courage or the foresight to do so. *What is he supposed to say to her?* He thinks but can't find an answer. He's not like Ahana's father—charming and caring and strong, or Aveek, brilliant and motivational. He's just a geek who's happy holding her hand, not someone who dates the prettiest girl there has ever been!

Aveek's the right boy for him, he concludes. He will not be around anyway and Ahana will find someone else to explore this city with, and who knows, she might be in Paris the next year, or in Brussels and will find someone better. *Who would want him?* he asks himself. Certainly not Ahana, who's funny, bright and so beautiful that it hurts.

# 25

Ranbeer can pay little attention to the manual of the new aircraft, the 486, and spends most of his time thinking about Sadhika and what she must be doing in Hong Kong. It's been a few months since they have been talking on and off, but lately, there are days when they don't talk about losing their partners and the hardships of raising a kid alone, and they *still* have plenty to talk about. It's been years since Ranbeer has had another friend.

He clears the security checks and checks in with his company for his test flight. He just has fifteen minutes to prepare himself for the flight. Sadhika calls him to make sure he's up to speed regarding his preparations.

'It's easy for you,' Sadhika says, her tone almost flirtatious.

'It will be easy because I know you will be on the other side of the radio,' he says, trying to be charming. It's been more than twelve years since he has wanted to say something that might impress a woman, let alone his colleague.

'Too kind,' she says.

The engineers at the test hangar strap him inside the aircraft, and Sadhika is on the radio on the other side, guiding him through the checks. He can barely suppress a smile, thinking how for the first time in years, the voice of another woman brings relief. As the controls of his cockpit light up around him, he decides he would ask her out on a proper date. As he rounds up the final checks, he wonders if he has a shirt he can wear on a date. He is adept at dressing up his daughter like a model, but he sticks to T-shirts and jeans. A black shirt would do just fine, he tells himself, already feeling nervous and shaky. Ahana likes Sadhika too, which gives him confidence.

'Can I have a word with the chief test engineer in private?' he asks. 'Sadhika Samant?'

'Cutting all lines,' the radio controller says.

'Can you hear me?' he asks.

'Crystal clear. Do you have some doubts? You know the routine, right?' she asks, concerned.

'I could have asked questions about the routine without asking people to stay off the line,' he says and takes a deep breath; his heart is pounding. 'I wish to take you out on a date when I'm back in Hong Kong. Can I?'

'Umm . . .'

'I asked a question.'

'Sure!' Sadhika mumbles nervously.

And then there is an awkward silence.

'I will see you when you're back,' Sadhika says, rather shyly.

'Looking forward, ma'am,' he says.

The radio connections are back again. The air traffic controller gives him clearance to fly. He closes his eyes and prays for her daughter's well-being, and thanks God for everything. He thinks about Sadhika. After a final check, he guides the aircraft to the runway, turns on the power, and winks at the picture of Farah that he keeps on the controls.

The aircraft lifts off, and the wheels retract inside. Little did he know that the wheels would never come down, again.

Sadhika is in the control room, watching the red and blue lights, the tiny graphs drawing themselves on the charts of paper, taking notes, but she's still shivering from the two-line conversation she just had with Ranbeer. She feels like a teenager, but she's sure it's nothing new for Ranbeer, who's used to reducing women to a mumbling mess of nerves.

*Concentrate! Concentrate!* she tells herself.

As the lights blink in front of her, she can't help but think of the hard times she has gone through without a single ray of hope to help her carry on, and of the man who wears T-shirts like he's still twenty-five years old, who just asked her, a mother of an eight-year-old, on a date. She's excited! This would be her first date, since her marriage was an outcome of an elaborate arranged set-up where the parents met first, horoscopes were matched and then over a single coffee shop meeting both the parties were expected to say a yes to marriage.

She starts wondering what she should wear on the date. Black would be flattering, she thinks. She needs to shop.

Just land this plane, she thinks to herself, and Ahana and she would go out shopping for her date with her father.

Little did she know she would never get to buy a dress for her first date.

26

Deep is back in Ahana's hotel room, sitting on her bed, while Ahana is on the piano pressing random keys. Today has been strange. Ahana, usually chirpy, and sometimes cranky, has been neither. She's been mostly quiet, hardly uttering any words, and even her fingers didn't reciprocate to his caressing them.

'Do you need some time alone?' he asks. Ahana nods. Deep leaves the room.

Ahana buries herself under the duvet, fighting her feelings for Deep, fearing rejection, scared that he would laugh at her for even thinking that there was a possibility that a normal boy would want to be with her. But surely, he has felt it too. A part of her believes that he knows they are more than friends, and he's a far cry from Aveek. Deep has had far more chances to kiss her, and Ahana knows she wouldn't have resisted.

Lying in her bed, she constructs an elaborate scenario

where she tells Deep what he is to her, and Deep understands. Every time she imagines that, she also imagines him telling her that though he likes her, they belong to different worlds, and they can't be together. And though she is broken in her daydream, she finds the strength to carry on in her life because she's glad he understands.

She's still lost in her constructs when the phone rings.

'Hello? Who's this?' she asks.

'Hi, Ahana, it's Sadhika. Are you in your hotel right now?' she asks, her voice broken and softer than she had last heard.

'Yes, I am. What happened?'

'I don't know how to put this, darling, but I know you should be the first to know—we've lost all radio contact with him . . .' she says nervously.

'WHAT?' Ahana shudders. 'What do you mean you have lost all radio contact with him?'

There is silence and she can hear her breath. 'He was on a test flight and ten minutes into the flight, the radio communication broke down. We are looking for him.'

Ahana's stomach churns and almost instantly she feels like puking. The words Sadhika just said hang in the air around her, echoing.

'Ahana, are you okay?' Sadhika asks concernedly.

She wasn't okay. Her feet buckle and she falls on the ground, her eyes are open, and her breathing is laboured and shallow. She's still clutching the phone, Sadhika's screams echoing through the receiver. She can hear, 'Are you there? Are you there, Ahana?' from the other end, but she lies paralysed on the ground, Sadhika's words wrapped around her neck, choking her, and she's frothing, struggling for breath, and the words don't leave her.

*Lost all radio contact. Lost all radio contact. We are looking for him. We are looking for him.*

She keeps saying these words under her breath, trying to understand the implications, trying to run away from them. It's her dad. *What do they mean, no radio contact? What do they mean they are looking for him?*

She brings the phone to her ear again. Her entire body is revolting and disintegrating, rejecting the words Sadhika has just said.

'AHANA! ARE YOU THERE?' Sadhika is still screaming. 'I have sent you a car. It will pick you up and get you to the office. We are doing the best we can.' Sadhika's voice is betraying her reassuring words.

'YOU'RE LYING! YOU'RE LYING!' Ahana screams and she throws the receiver, which hits the closest wall and spills to the ground. Screaming and crying, she runs out of her hotel room, miscounts the steps and collides with the door of the elevator. She rides it all the way down, crying and sobbing, the words turning her brain into mush. *Everything is okay*, she tells herself as she walks to the hotel lobby and then outside. *I just need to get to the office and confront Sadhika and find Dad.*

She has forgotten her cane in the hotel room, but it's too late, and she has already started running in the direction of her dad's office, barefoot and without her cane. She's running, she's running, trying to remember where she's going, trying to push Sadhika's words out of her head, the smiling face of her father flashes in her mind, the face she last saw when she was five, and she's crying. And then she's crashes against a pole and falls headlong on the ground.

She starts bleeding from her elbows, one of her legs feels

like it's broken, and she screams for help, but it's late in the night and she can feel the quietness around her. She doesn't know where she is and there seems to be nobody around. She keeps weeping, the blood trickles from her elbows to her palm. She feels like dying, that very moment, she wants to die and never come back. She's alone, she's all alone, lying on the street bleeding, while her father's lost in the radio silence somewhere. She's crying. She slams her fists against the pavement as her legs fail to support her when she tries to stand up.

Minutes pass by and she's sick and weak and bleeding, wailing and lying alone on the pavement. Her mind's playing tricks and she's passing in and out of consciousness. Then slowly she comes to and finds her cell phone in her pocket and thanks her stars. She calls her hotel and asks the man on the front desk to connect her to Deep.

'Ahana? Where are you?' Deep asks. He can only hear her wailing. 'Are you okay? Where are you?' He asks again.

'DAD!' she screams.

'What? What happened?'

'He's GONE!' she howls. '*THEY CAN'T FIND HIM!*'

'Where are you?' Deep asks and she only replies in wails. It takes him ten attempts to get a brief idea of the direction Ahana had run towards. He runs out of the hotel, frantic and scared. He can't help the tears that flood his eyes and blur his vision. His body's giving away and he's trying not to think about *He's gone* and *They can't find him*. *What does that mean?*

After walking fifteen minutes, he spots Ahana sprawled on the ground, breathing heavily, her eyes barely open; he can spot blood all over her. She's holding her leg and sobbing.

'Ahana! Wake up!' he slaps her face but she's just moaning and whispering the word *Dad*. 'Where's the office? WHERE IS THE OFFICE?' he shouts into her ear. She gives him her Dad's business card.

He waves to a taxi, and gingerly carries her into it. She's still only half-conscious, crying and begging Deep to take her to her dad.

'He will be okay,' he keeps repeating and running her hands over her face. She punches Deep's chest repeatedly. Deep doesn't have the courage to ask her what happened, and he tries to stay strong and not cry with her.

The car reaches the front of the building and he helps her get down from the cab. She shrieks in pain as she puts her feet to the ground. He supports her on his shoulders and they walk slowly towards the building. He keeps saying soothing words to her but she is stammering and sobbing.

After placing Ahana in a wheelchair, the guard takes them straight to the twelfth floor. As Deep walks into the waiting room, pushing the wheelchair in front of him, Sadhika is already there, along with two of her colleagues, and she has tears in her eyes.

# 27

Sadhika runs to Ahana, who steps out of the wheelchair and falls on the ground, wailing, her voice cracking. Her shouts are inaudible; her mouth opens wide but there's no sound, just an empty shriek of horror and despair. Sadhika motions at her colleague to get a doctor. She sits on the ground and wraps her arms around Ahana, who buries her head in Sadhika's chest and cries. Sadhika, whose face looks tired and dead and pale, runs her hand through Ahana's hair and keeps whispering into her ears. Only Deep can see that she looks broken herself.

He can't bear watching Ahana like this, on the floor, bleeding and crying.

Sadhika helps Ahana lie on the ground while the doctor tends to her wounds. He dresses up the cuts and the bruises on her elbows, and inspects her leg. Ahana winces when he touches her ankle, and Sadhika slaps the doctor's hand away. 'Later!' she snaps from behind her teary eyes and the doctor walks away. Sadhika keeps rocking Ahana in her arms, whispering and mumbling into her ears, kissing her from time to time, saying it will all be okay, lying that her father would be back soon. Hope and happiness lie crumpled on the floor in front of Deep and he's distraught, helpless and angry.

Deep is furious at the pointlessness of it all. He blames her father. *Why did he have to fly planes for a living?* He feels like grabbing Ranbeer by his throat and chide him for being an irresponsible father, slap him, and maybe bring him to life. *Such an asshole!* Deep thinks, with his swanky bike, that charming smile, the endearing demeanour and the fancy, faulty planes. He's so angry he can kill someone.

An hour passes by but it is as if the news just broke of her father's disappearance. Sadhika and Ahana are still wrapped around each other, the rhythm of their sobs now resonating. Sadhika's colleague, a man in his early thirties, walks in and asks if Sadhika can spare a moment. Sadhika's eyes widen, Ahana is all ears. The bad news is finally here, Deep thinks, and sits near them. Sadhika staggers to her feet, asks Deep to hold Ahana and walks out of the room with the colleague.

Deep holds her hand again and looks into Ahana's mourning eyes, which are screaming for someone to save her. He feels the world as they know it is coming to an end.

Going missing and gone are two very different situations, and Deep knows that as they wait for Sadhika to deliver the bad news. He feels like he's holding someone who's already dead; she's slowly disintegrating into pieces in his arms, he can feel her breath giving away, her soul draining out of her petite body.

The door opens and Sadhika walks in through them. Deep's eyes are stuck on her, ready to face the worst.

Sadhika sighs. She says, 'The jerk is alive!'

Ahana looks in her direction, tears streaming down, confusion written all over her face. Sadhika adds happily, 'Your dad is alive, Ahana! He's unhurt and is on a plane back to Hong Kong!'

'FUCK!' Deep mouths out aloud. Sadhika bends down and Ahana jumps into her arms like a ninja and they are laughing and crying all at once. Then they are kissing each other all over, and Sadhika is saying, 'I told you he would be okay . . . I told you he would be okay . . .' and Ahana is saying, 'I hate him so much! I hate him so much!' Everyone in the room is crying and smiling, including the doctor and Sadhika's colleagues and Deep, all of them shaking hands and hugging and high-fiving each other.

'The bastard ejected the aircraft at the last moment, right before it exploded. Not a scratch!' the colleague says.

'NO ONE calls him that,' Ahana snaps. 'Maybe *she* can,' she adds and points towards Sadhika.

'I would never call him that!' Sadhika says and hugs Ahana tighter.

'Can *I*?' Deep asks, quietly. 'I really want to.'

'Just this one time,' Ahana says.

'That bastard!'

Everyone laughs.

Deep, Sadhika and Ahana sit around in a tight circle waiting to hear from Ranbeer. They are smiling. Ahana has not stopped grinning, and every few seconds she breaks out laughing and saying, 'This is the best day of my life, forever.'

And then they laugh.

Three hours pass by, in which Ahana and Deep tease Sadhika like she's a teenager, and she shyly smiles like one. They ask her about Varun, her eight-year-old son, of whom she shows pictures on her phone and Deep goes, 'Aww!' For Ahana she plays a video of Varun talking and Ahana finds his voice cute and adorable. The doctor bandages Ahana's foot and tells them that it's just a sprain, and Ahana says she can't even feel any pain any more.

It's not until four in the morning that Ranbeer barges in through the door and Ahana leaps up and limps to him, almost missing him, but Ranbeer picks her up and kisses her all over her face.

'DARE YOU DO THAT AGAIN!' Ahana screams and hits him wherever she can.

'I'm so sorry, I'm so sorry. I promise,' Ranbeer keeps saying, and looks over her shoulder towards Sadhika, who's crying as well, her hands over her mouth, looking so beautiful. Slowly, Sadhika walks up to Ranbeer and kisses Ahana on her head.

'It's not just me who wants to kill you now that you're alive,' Ahana whispers in her father's ears. Both Ranbeer and Sadhika smile shyly.

'Don't you ever do that, ever!' Sadhika says, her eyes welling up again.

'I never intended to miss our date,' he replies and then they hug each other.

Deep just looks from a distance and cries before Ahana calls him over and they all have a group hug. Deep and Sadhika tell the father–daughter pair that they need to rest but they are in no mood to listen.

'I JUST GOT MY DAD BACK!' Ahana exclaims.

'AND I JUST GOT BACK FROM THE DEAD! I NEED A DRINK!' he shouts enthusiastically.

'But we need to get to the bottom of this,' Sadhika says, concerned. 'Did the technical team tell you what went wrong? I mean someone has to be—'

Ranbeer puts a finger on her lips to shut her up and tells her it's a conversation for some other day. Ahana joins in to insist on the need to celebrate the day and Deep and Sadhika's words fall to deaf ears.

It's four-thirty but they know of a place which is open 24 x 7. They catch a cab to the clubbing district, to the place where it isn't dawn till it is, for the flashy lights of Hong Kong calls out to them.

The grown-ups drink themselves silly that night. Ranbeer drinks like a tanker and forces Sadhika to join in. They hop from one bar to another, dancing like there's no tomorrow. Only after they have exhausted themselves, they return to their hotel after finding a cab for Sadhika. It's only Deep who's still in his senses and Ahana is piggy-backing on his shoulder. He helps Ranbeer to his bed in their suite, and then he makes the bed for Ahana. Ahana wraps her arms around his neck, pulling his face near hers, lips slightly parted.

Deep gently breaks out from her embrace and tells her, 'I would want you to remember our first kiss together,' and adds after a second, 'forever.'

She falls asleep before he can tell her that he has a flight back to New Delhi next morning.

# Part Four

# The Nerd Boy

# 28

The aircraft touches down at the Indira Gandhi International Airport, and while I fill up the immigration form, I'm hoping I fill it up wrong and that they send me back to Hong Kong, a place I have come to love so much that I want to be deported from my own country right now. The immigration officer stamps on my passport, and I'm furious at the incompetency of government officials. I had spelt my name wrong. For heaven's sake, send me back! Send me back!

I didn't think I would miss Hong Kong as much. I knew my brain would explode because missing Ahana is like dying, only I am living. The pain is almost physical, and as I tread towards the conveyor belt, I'm thinking of the narrow roads, the eighteen-tyre trucks that don't jam the roads, the tops of the buildings I could never see, the calmness of Tai O, the madness of the pubs and the bars, the sophisticated surroundings of the SoHo district that made me want to dress up in fine clothes and drink wine and dance. I miss being in the city where history is sold in quaint little shops on Hollywood Road, the city that obscures your views about how the old and the new can co-exist and thrive. I miss the food, I miss the energy, and I miss everything I have done in the past few days, which now looks like a montage of pictures from another life.

My suitcase is the last one on the belt, which is okay by me, because as long as I'm in the airport, I can still fly to Hong Kong and hug Ahana and revisit all the places I had with her. And maybe even settle down in one of the huts in Tai O, or nestle on the top floor of a seventy-five-storey building with a view of the harbour. God! I miss her! And I miss Hong Kong!

I walk with my head hung low, and slowly walk towards the exit. There are hundreds of eyes on me, wondering if I am their own, and I'm looking back at them with the same question in my eyes.

'DEEP!' Mom shouts as soon as I exit from the Arrivals gate. I walk towards her, as my father tries to hold her steady. With them stand my buddies—Aman and Manasi. Mom is slowly dissolving into tears and she lunges at me like it's the sudden death of the World Cup final. 'You have become so weak! You have become so weak!' she says and caresses my face with her hands and kisses me. She just can't stop crying.

Manasi leans over and whispers in Mom's ear, 'He is alive, Aunty. I told you he's alive.'

Aman and Dad laugh.

There's a taxi waiting. Aman is riding shotgun and Mom's close to me, still crying, still kissing me, and telling me how weak I have become, and Dad's asking me about how Hong Kong was and I just can't shut up about it.

'You and Mom should go some time. It's great! You will fall in love with that place,' I am gushing.

Before Dad can respond, Mom interjects, 'Go to Hong

Kong? What will you do here alone? I'm not going anywhere without you. What will you eat?' And she starts sobbing again. Everyone else is laughing.

'Fine. Fine. I will come along too. I don't mind at all!' I answer.

'So, Deep,' Manasi says. 'Besides work for the library, what else did you do? Did you get inspiration for your book there? Or did you just keep wandering like a lost, homeless boy?'

'Kind of both, mostly the latter, but I think I can write a trilogy!' I mock.

I know Aman has been dying to ask me his questions, which I'm certain would revolve around girls and parties, but he stays quiet till the time we reach my house. Nostalgia is a strong feeling, and I feel euphoric as I enter my own room. There's a sense of calm that flows over me. I'm ecstatic for a few minutes, but after that as I get used to my room again, I'm back to being anxious. I'm wondering if I would ever see her again, and would she remember me, or would she take someone else to all the places we had been to, and let someone else hold her hand, slip his fingers into hers. It sucks.

'So?' Aman asks when the three of us are on our own.

'Yes, yes, there were plenty of hot women and girls all around the city. You will love that place,' I mock.

'I know I will love the place, but did you? Did you get lucky?' he looks at me with his charming, yet totally creepy eyes.

'If by "lucky" you mean did I find the love of my life? Someone I don't think I will stop thinking about even when I'm eighty and when you will have herpes and you're on the death bed hitting on nurses one-third your age, then maybe!'

'What do you mean I will get herpes?' Aman protests. 'I'm like the poster boy of safe sex. Oh! Wait.'

'Did you just say you fell in love?' Manasi, who up till now was just gawking at Aman, butts in.

'Do you want to see pictures?' I ask and fish out my laptop, not because I want them to see her, but because I want to see her myself.

I click on the Hong Kong folder, which I have backed up on five different online photo-sharing sites, just in case, and there are around thirteen thousand pictures of her.

'DAMN!' Aman shrieks.

'Is that her?' Manasi asks. 'You were just stalking her, weren't you? Tell me you're stalking her. You can't be in love with her. She's gorgeous! She's like one-third Anne Hathaway, mixed with one-third each of Emma Watson and Jennifer Lawrence. And you're just a tall Danny De Vito.'

'This is INSANE,' Aman butts in. 'EPIC INSANE.' You can always count on Aman to make grammatically incorrect phrases sound cool.

'Hey,' Manasi notes, 'why isn't she looking into the camera in any of the pictures. She is beautiful and everything, but is she, like, also squint?'

'She's blind,' I answer.

Their faces go blank and I wait for them to register the news. They want details. I tell them everything from the first day to the last and looking at the pictures, they piece together a timeline in their heads, and they end up patting me and feeling happy for me.

'You're so full of shit, Deep,' Manasi says. 'You just fooled a blind girl into falling in love with you. Imagine if she can see you tomorrow. She will run faster than Usain Bolt. Gone in a second!'

'Oh, shut up,' Aman argues and puts his arm around my

shoulder and squeezes me. 'Our boy is good-looking, too! I don't know about you, but I'm hungry and I need to eat,' he says and leaves the room.

'Manasi? Do you really think she will leave me when she sees me? If ever?' I ask nervously.

'Is there a chance?'

'There is. She told me once. There's a gene therapy treatment. It's long and unreliable, but there's a chance,' I tell her.

'Deep, I know you're hideous and all, and even if you were the last boy on earth, I wouldn't consider you, not even for a bit, but you're a really nice guy. It seems like she genuinely likes you. She has been blind almost all her life. Do you think how you *look* would matter to her?' she assures me.

'I love you,' I respond.

'Whatever. What did you get for me?' she asks. And when I shake my head, she hits me furiously.

'I'm sorry.'

'I forgive you. You were busy with her. When are you making us meet her?' she asks.

'I wish I knew,' I answered.

Mom walks into my room and asks us to join Aman on the dining table and we do so, lest she starts crying again.

Manasi whispers in my ear, 'I want to read the book you write on her if you ever do.'

I nod.

# 29

It's been three months since I've been back in Delhi, and my life sucks big time with a capital S, capital U, capital C, capital K, capital S. SUCKS. There isn't a single day when I don't miss her, and curse myself for not having missed that flight, for not telling her the night before that I was leaving. Maybe they would have woken up from their exhausted slumber and would have seen me off. Maybe it would have made me miss her less, but then again, who am I kidding? I would have only missed her more.

Not that she ever lets me forget her. We talk on the phone day in and day out, but it's never enough. Nothing can compare to the days I spent walking around, holding her hands, wishing time would stop and lock that moment forever.

'Dude!' Aman slaps my back as I'm swimming in the watery ketchup of my college canteen, trying to drown my miseries in it. 'You're still mourning over her? You spend hours on Skype every day, man. Your longing is worse than a woman's.'

'Like seriously, Deep,' Manasi adds, who has lost quite some weight since the time Aman broke up with his girlfriend. 'It's not like she's dead or something. She's just blind.'

'Oh, shut up with your blind jokes!' I protest. 'Or on the other hand, can you please keep talking about her. Keep taking her name, too, it's Ahana. Say it over and over again, till it's the only sound I can hear.'

'I would rather die,' Manasi says and eats a french fry off my plate.

'If you eat one more of those, I will make sure you do!' I snap and snatch the plate away from her. She has to stick to her diet.

'Though I have to admit it, Deep, she's so pretty,' Aman points out.

'Are *you* telling *me*? I KNOW THAT!' I retort.

'God!' Manasi exclaims. 'It's like you've been PMSing for the last three months!'

'That reminds me of her,' I say. 'She once said that being blind is like PMSing for a lifetime.'

'Enough,' Manasi puts her foot down. 'I don't have time for this lovelorn Romeo. I have a class to attend. Are you coming, Aman?'

'Right behind you,' he says.

There's a definite change in the power balance between Aman and Manasi. Aman, the college stud, strangely acquiesces to every demand put forward by Manasi, but I have no time to think about them. I have to mourn the distance between Ahana and me and be insecure about the boys around her.

I sleep through IT Architecture, Advanced JAVA and C++, as I travel back to Hong Kong, to its brightly lit streets, walking past the billboards of every fashion brand conceivable, dodging well-dressed men and women, clutching Ahana's hand tightly in mine ... she's tapping my shoulder and saying, 'Deep, Deep, Deep. Wake up. Wake up.'

*Wake up? Wake up?*

I wake up with a start and I'm sure I have gone crazy because what I see can't be true. She's right there, sitting next to me, looking towards at me, but not quite, smiling, and just sitting like she's not the love of my life.

'Wh ... wh ... what are you doing here?'

'Shouldn't I be asking you the same question? You should be in class,' she says, her eyes full of mischief.

'How are you here? How did you find me?'

'Don't worry. I'm sure Dad is looking at us from his viewfinder from the top of a nearby building,' she laughs.

'Can I like, hug you?'

'I would if you don't!' she shrieks and we hug and my eyes fill up and she just goes 'Awww!'

'What took you so long? It took you three months to come and meet me?' I growl.

'At least I'm not like you, going away unannounced, the very day I wanted to tell you how much I loved you!' she retorts, still looking at my eyes, which is strange.

'I'm so sorry!' I say. 'But believe me, I have had the temptation to sell off books from my father's library and buy the first ticket to Hong Kong. God! I missed you.' I hug her again.

'I missed you more. There wasn't a single second when I didn't think about you,' she purrs.

'But I'm still angry. It took you three months to come and see me. That's just cruel!' I grumble.

'I was busy,' she argues.

'Busy doing what? Learning to make clicking sounds like your ex-boyfriend!'

'Can you stop being jealous of him for, like, one second, Deep?' she asks, but she also smiles, which I don't miss.

'So what were you busy with?' I ask.

'I was busy relearning all the things I had unlearned,' she says.

'Stop with the riddles.'

'I was busy looking at our pictures,' she explains.

'Looking at our pictures?' I smirk. 'They come in Braille now?'

'Oh, stop being an ass. I mean real pictures,' she says. 'That's what people who can see get clicked for, right? So that they can look at their pictures later?'

'I don't get you,' I snap irritably. 'You've got to stop being cryptic. It takes away your cuteness.'

'The treatment I told you about? Where they had to dig through my optic nerve and cut close to my brain and shift a few things here and there, well, it worked a little. It was a pretty badass surgery and I was brave as hell during it. Even Dad agrees. I can see a little now, Deep.'

'What are you saying?'

'I'm saying that I can see how cute you are, I can see that you're tall, a little too tall for me, but I will make do. I'm saying that I can see how your face resembles like that of a puppy when you look at me, something that Dad always told me, and I can see that I'm hopelessly, irrevocably in love with you,' she says.

'Umm . . . you can see me?' I ask, my eyes widen, my brain processes what it saw in the mirror this morning.

'Not clearly. I have these big glasses I have to wear to see clearly, but I can make out your silhouette,' she explains.

'Wear your glasses!' I tell her and she puts on her black-rimmed nerdy glasses, and she looks like a really cute kindergarten teacher.

'You're so out of my league now!' I protest. 'Your blindness is all that was in my favour.'

'Now that I can see you, I think I like you better,' she replies.

'I don't believe girls who can see. They often lie.' I take her glasses off. 'This is much better. You will always be a midnight girl in my book, blind as a bat.'

'Are you writing it?'

'I just finished the first bit. It's set in my favourite city, Hong Kong, and my favourite person is in it,' I answer.

'I will not try to guess who that favourite person is,' she responds and adds after a pause, 'Can I now get my kiss that I'm supposed to remember forever?'

'Here?' I ask nervously, looking around.

'Looks like a good place for a forever to start,' she says and leans into me.

Our lips touch, and it feels like death, it feels like life, it feels like the streets of Hong Kong, it feels like the lights, the skyscrapers, like the touch of her hands, like the despair of a helpless girl, like the happiness of reading, it feels like everything; and from the corner of my eye, I can see her dad, watching and smiling. Without a gun in his hand, but instead, a smiling Sadhika by his side.

Latest by DURJOY

*The Boy Who Loved*

**The only thing you cannot plan in life is when and
who to fall in love with . . .**

Raghu likes to show that there is nothing remarkable
about his life—loving, middle-class parents, an elder
brother he looks up to, and plans to study in an IIT.
And that's how he wants things to seem—normal.

Deep down, however, the guilt of letting his closest friend
drown in the school's swimming pool gnaws at him. And
even as he punishes himself by hiding from the world and
shying away from love and friendship, he feels drawn to the
fascinating Brahmi—a girl quite like him, yet so different.
No matter how hard Raghu tries, he begins to care . . .

Then life throws him into the deep end and he has
to face his worst fears.

Will love be strong enough to pull him out?

*The Boy Who Loved*, first of a two-part romance,
is warm and dark, edgy and quirky, wonderfully
realistic and dangerously unreal.

*Releasing May 2017*